Yar

by

JOHN JORDAN

POOLBEG PRESS: DUBLIN

This collection first published 1977 by Poolbeg Press Ltd.,
Knocksedan House, Swords, Co. Dublin, Ireland.

Cover: Jarlath Hayes

Printed by The Leinster Leader Ltd., Naas, Co. Kildare

Acknowledgments are due to the editors of *Arena, New Irish Writing* (The Irish Press), *Kilkenny Magazine, St. Stephen's, University Review, Best Irish Short Stories* (Paul Elek Ltd.) *Dublin Magazine,* and *Dolmen Miscellany,* in which most of the stories in this collection first appeared.

Contents

The generous assistance of An Chomhairle Ealaion in the publication of this book is gratefully acknowledged.

For

CHRISTINE LONGFORD

*Who remembers reading the earliest
of these stories
thirty years ago*

and

EDWARD CONE

*In memory of
Salzburg, many other places,
and RPB*

September 1939

Brother Hennessy's normal voice was quiet and coarse: it reminded Fintan of the sensation he felt when he let his boot slide across gravel. Brother Hennessy's face, in repose, had the helplessness of an old horse turned out to die. His eyes, though, when examined closely, showed wan flickers of malevolence: the old horse might yet, and indeed did, kick hard and dangerously.

Already that morning, before prayers, he had given Jimmy Riordan six on each hand with the strap. He had found him copying tots from Fintan's exercise book. Fintan himself had got away with three and a swipe on the behind. He stood now with Jimmy on the 'line', as they called the strip of floor between the desks and the inner wall of the classroom. Jimmy was very pale, and he clenched his swollen hands tightly against his worn corduroy shorts. Fintan was shocked, and faintly disgusted, to see that Jimmy's eyes were brimming, and that down one cheek, one large tear was slowly advancing.

Brother Hennessy, for all his awakened viciousness, seemed in good humour. He blew his nose in a large snuff-bloodier handkerchief, sneezed out of the window, took a couple of gallops up and down the space in front of his desk, and finally got up on it, slipping his strap into the pocket of his gown. He was smiling.

'Boys,' he began, and stopped, apparently overcome by the burden of his announcement.

'Lads', he tried again, and smiled more horribly. A little

7

stream of blackish fluid was making for his upper lip. He
must have taken snuff at the window.

'Lads,' he rasped decisively, 'this is an historic morning.'

It was the adjective which brought them to attention.
They left off scratching legs that smarted from overtight
garters, picking noses that already scented the coming
winter, rubbing palms that instinctively prepared for
punishment. They had heard the word 'historic' before. It
had to do with the 'past' and the 'past' meant pitch-capped
children, and martyred priests, and mysterious Protestant
heroes like Wolfe Tone and Robert Emmet. The 'past' they
must all be proud of, since it was then that they Kept the
Faith and Broke the Connection with England.

'Yes,' said Brother Hennessy. 'An historic morning.
Germany has invaded Poland!'

His balloon deflated. Forty sleep-ringed pairs of eyes
stared back at him. Germany they'd heard of, but
Poland was as remote from them as Timbuctoo.

Brother Hennessy stopped smiling. He got down from his
desk, and walked across to Jimmy Riordan in a way Fintan
had never before seen, friskly, jauntily, as if at any moment he
might skip in the air and do some kind of jig.

'Do you know what that means?' he rasped at Jimmy.

'I don't, sir ... I mean, yes ...'

'Out with it, man, or I'll knock the hide off you.'

'Well, sir, it might mean a war.'

Brother Hennessy gave Jimmy's ear a routine tug, and
went back to his paddock.

'Yes, lads, *that's* what it means, a war.'

They'd had a war in Spain, Fintan could remember.
Priests and nuns had been murdered. He wondered if the
Christian Brothers had been let off. He even admitted the
fancy that Brother Hennessy would be murdered. But his
mother had told him that Brother Hennessy was a very holy
man who did his duty.

'Yes,' crooned Brother Hennessy. 'It'll be Germany
against England.'

'Who'll win, sir?' shrilled Fatser Mulcahy.

'Who'll win?'

It was as if someone had questioned the existence of God or Our Lady. Brother Hennessy's nostrils flared, his weak old eyes flamed, his hands came out of his shiny chalk-stained robe, and Fintan tensed himself for one of Brother Hennessy's famous onslaughts.

These onslaughts were infrequent but all-inclusive, and practically no-one escaped while the fury was on: hands, backs, bottoms, thighs, were attacked, and once Fatser Mulcahy got a clout on the ear, so that it bled. Brother Hennessy had patted Fatser on the head afterwards, and told him he was a good boy. Fatser's mother had gone to the Superior.

But Brother Hennessy controlled himself.

'Spelling,' he roared.

Later in the morning, Fintan looked across at Jimmy's bowed head. He found it hard to understand why Jimmy, so brave, so proud, should be upset by a few biffs. Their code required that legitimate punishment be accepted without murmur. Odds were not weighed in the war with authority and, if one lost, one paid without question the price of a welted palm or a deafened ear. Of course it was different if blood was drawn, and all the boys said it was very unfair when Fatser Mulcahy's ear bled, and the Superior gave cheek to his Ma.

At the half-hour break, he saw Jimmy sitting by himself in the playground shelter. His penny bottle of milk and his packet of bread-and-jam lay beside him on the seat. Fintan was moving slowly across to him, driven by pity, held back by shyness and distaste, when he saw Ben Lucy run up to Jimmy. Ben was the biggest boy in the class. He had glasses and red hair, and he liked to punch the smaller boys and threaten to take down their trousers.

'Cry-baby,' he said to Jimmy.

Fintan was flabbergasted when Jimmy stayed still and silent. That was going too far. He turned away in disgust. And then he heard Ben Lucy's howl of pain. Jimmy had him on the ground and he was pulling his hair mercilessly. Out of the corner of his eye, Fintan saw Brother Hennessy taking an amble in their direction.

'Ay, nix!' he shouted.

Jimmy rolled off Ben Lucy, who was blubbering by this time. Fintan pulled Jimmy away, and in a moment they were sitting together, eating their bread-and-jam and drinking their milk.

'I don't care if Lousy Lucy tells oul' Hennessy,' said Jimmy.

'Why should you?' said Fintan, and hesitantly, 'you're not a cry-baby, anyway.'

'I wasn't crying because I was biffed,' said Jimmy defiantly.

'I know that, Riordan.'

And then Jimmy blurted out what Fintan was too shy to ask.

'I seen the paper before I came to school, at least me Ma did. Me Da's in the British Army, and me Ma says he'll be killed if there's a war.'

'I have no Da,' was all Fintan could find to say in comfort.

The bell clanged out. Jimmy leaped up and ran to the lavatory, his hob-nailed boots striking sparks from the asphalt. Tangles of boys sorted out and formed into lines. Once around the playground and in, was the usual routine. To-day, Brother Hennessy took them round twice. 'Left, right, left, right,' he rasped in Irish, and his little soldiers were happy in their additional minute's freedom. But Jimmy was late.

They were already settled at their desks for English Composition on the Life of an Old Donkey, when he came rushing in. Brother Hennessy seized him by the scruff and threw him spinning.

'Hold out,' he raved. He'd been snuffing again, and the blackish fluid was thick and gleaming between lip and nostril.

Jimmy held out both palms, after rubbing on his trouser-seat. Then the strap came down, twelve times in all. They expected that that would be the end. There was a long, mournful gasp from the class when Brother Hennessy pulled Jimmy towards him and took the fat from one cheekbone in his veined and mottled hands.

'Where were you?' he hissed.

'I . . . I was in the lavatory, sir. I . . . I had a pain.'

'Pain?' said Brother Hennessy kindly.

'Yes, sir, a pain.'

'I'll give you a pain,' said Brother Hennessy. He might have been offering Jimmy a penny for sweets.

The first two blows had come down, when Fintan screamed, and jumped from his desk. He hurled himself at the astonished Brother, and dragged downwards on his wearied old arms. He began to kick at Brother Hennessy's shins, and as he kicked he babbled.

'Ah leave him alone, sir, leave him alone, his Da's in the English Army, sir, and he's going to be killed in the war and ah, sir, leave him alone'.

Brother Hennessy began to bray and sob.

'Get Brother Superior,' he howled. 'Get Brother Superior, there's a mad boy here, a mad boy.'

But Fintan fell away by himself, and he lay on the ground, crying. Jimmy came to him, picked him up, and gave him his filthy handkerchief. Brother Hennessy had a curious glassy look in his eyes. His lips were creamy with spittle. Suddenly he shuddered, and stooped for his fallen strap.

'Get up to the Superior,' they heard him rasp before he had risen.

'Get up to the Superior,' he rasped again. 'I'll be up after yous, yous young pups, yous slum-brats.'

They took each other by the hand, like little girls or lovers. They walked slowly along the dusty sunlit corridors. They could hear the chanting of lessons and, far off, the cracked voices of the big boys' singing class:

O Salutaris Hostia,
Quae coeli pandis ostium:
Bella premunt hostilia,
Da robur, fer auxilium.

As they climbed the stairs to the Superior's office, they did not once look at each other.

The Laburnum Queen

They showed no signs of leaving, even when the bells of the nearby Passionist Monastery rang the first Angelus of the day. They're a fine crowd, she thought grimly. Only Mr. Fox appeared to be moved by the bells. 'What are those bells?' he asked thickly. 'Those bloody bells'd drive you mad.'

'Those,' said Mrs. Fox savagely, 'are the bells of Mount Argus, and they're ringing the six o'clock Angelus: six o'clock on a fine sunny morning, and it's time you stopped soaking yourself.'

And turning to Charlie Dowling, she said, 'Charlie love, do you think my Johnny's out of sorts over some girl?'

Mr. Fox overheard. 'When there's a mot involved, the only escape is this,' and he pointed to the whiskey bottle on the floor beside him. He slumped then from his chair with a fat thud.

Oh thank God, she thought, now he's passed out, maybe we can get the rest of them to go. I'll get Charlie Dowling to help me to carry him upstairs, though he's a terrible weight poor man, God help him.

But her guests paid no attention while Mrs. Fox and Charlie dragged the drunken man to his feet, and slowly propped him to the door. Attention to Fox would mean distraction from the task of prolonging the night, of finishing the half-empty bottles of gin and whiskey, and, it was rumoured, three untouched dozen of stout. Without further help, Mrs. Fox and Charlie got the man upstairs, blocked only once on the landing, as Johnny came out of the bathroom. They stopped for a moment as he passed in front of them, and through the open skylight the thin first sunshine caught in brightness the boy and the drunken man. Oh Mother of God, she thought, how alike they are. Charlie Dowling was adroit and silent as they put Fox between the eiderdown and blankets. Only as they were coming down the stairs did he say to Mrs. Fox, 'No, I don't think it's a girl that has Johnny depressed.' She cocked her eye in what was meant to be a cunning manner, and he smiled kindly and knowingly.

The room seemed colder: this was before Mrs. Fox threw open the french-windows and let in the brisk new air. Making a final gesture before telling them all plainly to go to their homes if they'd any to go to, she switched off the light and stood by the door. But though her mouth opened to give them a good telling-off, she suddenly found herself shocked into silence. This is my room, she thought, the big cream-distempered room (the front reception-room, and she remembered how thrilled she had been at having a house with two reception-rooms) with the Paul Henry landscape and the Keating drawing of a fisherman, and the huge round mirror over the fireplace. Don't be daft, she told herself. But she remained at the door, staring at the tasteful green carpet powdered with cigarette ash and blobbed with stout-stains; the big old nuisance of a bookcase stuffed with Encyclopaedia Britannica and the calf-bound sets of Dickens and Thackeray, bought because poor Dickie had said they must have good reading-matter laid on for the kids; the chintz-covered chesterfield set piled now with sleepy amorous bodies in crumpled suits and blouses, people she hardly knew but who now seemed to her part of the furniture of her home, of what Dickie and she had made in twenty-five years.

Mrs. Fox shivered. There now, she thought, they're all all right, anyway it was a grand party ... only why wasn't Johnny there? Why had he stayed all night in his room? She hoped anyway he'd put on the gas-fire, the nights were cold even if the mornings were fine, and she always had a feeling about his chest. ... Then for the first time she noticed the

boy, a long skinny boy who was squatting on the floor,
pulling primroses from a little cut-glass bowl he must have
taken from the piano. She did not recognise him. He must,
she thought, have come with the Kennedys, or the
Gallaghers, or maybe he was a friend of Johnny's. That was
it, a friend of Johnny's. She began to walk across the room,
tripping over legs, intending to give him a late welcome, and
at the same time to scold him for destroying her lovely
primroses. But when she came close to him, she could find
nothing to say, because she saw he was crying. The gin, she
thought. Gin was a terrible thing for making people cry.
Many's a good cry she'd had herself over a drop of
Gordon's. Poor lamb. She lowered herself carefully to the
floor beside him and putting her hand on his arm, said,
'There now, pet, it'll be all right before you're twice married.'
She kept on saying this until the boy flummoxed her by
asking what the hell she meant. With an effort this time, she
said 'It'll be all right.' And presently the boy sat up and
asked for a drink.

'What's your name?' she asked.
'Matthew.'
Mrs. Fox giggled, and began to recite,
 'Matthew, Mark, Luke, and John
 Went to bed . . .'
but thought better of it.
'You know,' he said. 'You're quite beautiful.'
Automatically she tilted her chin and patted her hair at
the nape of her neck, before putting on a stern expression
and saying 'Now then, none of that nonsense.' All the same,
she was saddened. It might have been true once, she thought,
before poor Dickie, before Johnny . . . she felt angry
suddenly that she should have a cross like Johnny;
everything would be grand if only he'd get back some of his
nice ways as a little boy. And she remembered with pride
how fine he looked in his drill-display whites and how she
and Dickie had been told by a man they met in the pub that
Johnny would stand out anywhere, even in a bloody drill-
display! Oh how they'd laughed. She grew aware, and
indeed how could she imagine such a thing, that the bony

child who had told her she was beautiful was not her son, and that somewhere in the house was her own flesh and blood.

She got up and went out into the hall.

'Johnny,' she screamed, 'come down, love, come down.'

He heard her, from his room at the top of the house. He was lying on his bed, straight and quiet. His face felt hot and salty. He was thinking of a green half-lit wood in the Midlands where he had gone as a child with his parents, and he brushed away what might have been a tear or a remembered bird.

'Johnny, oh Johnny, come down, come down!'

She was baying now. All his life he could remember it. 'Johnny come in for your tea ...' The summer evenings when he had to leave the hide-and-seek, and the face-pulling at old Hawkins the Protestant as he mowed his lawn, scowling at them only when he stopped to sniff at his clumps of night-scented stock. 'Johnny, hurry up, we'll be late ...' The reverie in the bathroom ended and his hair still not sleeked, his ears still not clean. And she would come up for him, in her lemon hat and white shoes and brown woollen frock — always wool in summer, so that she sweated, and pulled at her hips; and always summer in his memories of her.

He heaved himself from the bed and made for the stairs. She was waiting for him at the bannister-end, her battered face, like a wrecked sand-castle, tilted appealingly. He could see her bosom heaving beneath the black satin party-frock. A faint smell of gin came to him as he approached her.

Mrs. Fox felt her throat thicken with tenderness: how thin the pet is, she thought, like an old scarecrow, thin as that Matthew. She fed timidly on the taut flesh beneath the pyjamas, the tousled mousy hair, the aggressive alien face.

'Johnny love,' she said. 'Are you all right? Why don't you slip on a few things and finish up the party with us? People will think it very strange you not making an appearance.'

'No thanks, Mammy. I'm tired.'

He turned back upstairs and she shouted after him, in a

melodramatic, hoarse voice, 'You're a terribly difficult boy.'

At last they were going. But she paid them little notice. Tiny things caught her attention, the bedraggled violets at May Kennedy's v-line, the gleam of somebody's lens, Billy Gallagher fastening his fly. When she had closed the door, she leaned back against it and rested. She heard the cars coughing, the sleepy hearty voices shouting 'Good-bye now' and 'Suppose I'll see you in Davy Byrne's before the week's out.'

The bells again. Seven o'clock Mass. A good party, and on the whole a nice crowd. Oh, she thought, I'm tired. I could lie down and die, I'm that tired. I thought they'd never go. You'd be killed running parties for a crowd like that. She opened the collar of her frock. I wonder is there a pick left in the house? They had the hunger in the heart, that lot, ham sandwiches, pickle-and-cheese, egg-and-tomato, the whole lot gone. And as far as I can see not a drop to drink is there left. Maybe the stout, Dickie would need that when he gets up. I'd better see what mess there is to clear up, and leave a note for Maggie. But when she looked in to see what work there would be for the maid, the room wasn't empty. Charlie Doyle was there, and Matthew. Charlie was nursing a half-full gin-bottle, a triumphant expression on his face, still looking sleek and talcumed. Matthew was still on the floor, his legs splayed out over the wrecked primroses. He was snoring.

'My God,' she said. 'Why are you still here?'

'I thought you might need some help with him,' said Charlie.

'Poor lamb,'she said. 'We'd better not disturb him. But then if we leave him on the floor, he'll catch his death.' She went over to Matthew and touched his head, smiling foolishly and kindly.

'Wake up,' she said. It's time to get going.'

His face trembled and his eyes opened. He groped in the air and said, 'My head.'

'All right then, we'll make you some good hot coffee, and then you'll be as right as rain. Come on now.'

The three of them moved in procession to the kitchen,

silent and solemn. Charlie went first, a little ahead, his small compact body erect and authoritative. Mrs. Fox followed, and behind her she could sense the boy and his hot sour breath on her neck. Boys, she thought, boys were strange creatures. Men she could understand. They were straight-forward for the most part, easy to handle once you got used to them. Like her own Dickie. Fond of the drink, fond of the bed, fond of a good greasy meal. But boys now, they were different. And she remembered things that had made her feel sad when she was young. Her father's face when he found out she'd stolen half-a-crown from his top-coat pocket, hearing the Tenebrae on Good Friday for the first time with her schoolfriend Susie Belton, the first kiss she'd ever had, from a carrot-haired young man in a tight blue suit on the Hill of Howth. Boys, she thought, would break your heart.

It was still half-light in the kitchen. A big lilac tree grew outside the window and kept out the sunshine. Mrs. Fox moved busily from dresser to stove, and from stove to table, and they were all silent until the coffee was steaming on the table.

Charlie began.

'The lilac is lovely,' he said.

That started her off. She talked on and on. She told them how all her life she had loved the lilac, how all her life the lilac had been her favourite, until the laburnum. Her grandmother had had a lilac tree in her garden, and in hot weather she would sit with her, and they'd press their faces in the cold purple flowers. She had brought Susie Belton to her grandmother's and under the lilacs for a whole summer they had talked about boys and girls and falling in love and getting married.

'I never thought then,' she said, 'that Susie would be the one to go into a convent and me the one to marry and have a big lad of my own.'

Suddenly she stopped and listened. But Johnny was asleep in his room, dreaming of the Midlands wood, where he fought bright birds, and found himself suddenly naked among the trees, ashamed, lost, listening for the voice which would ask him, sooner or later, where his clothes were.

Yes, she told them, she had always loved the lilac. But then the laburnum. She thought she loved that even more. She had loved it for years now, ever since Johnny had made her a big streeling crown of it, and said, 'Mammy, you're the Laburnum Queen.' It was at the end of the garden, the laburnum tree, and sometimes when it was in blossom, she'd sit under it, and honest to God, it was grand,, and all that yellow pouring down around her.

'Matthew,' she said. 'That's your name isn't it? — if ever you count your days by your granny's lilac, and an old laburnum, then you'll have good reason to cry, you silly lad. But sure I'm silly myself to be talking on like this.'

'I'm tired,' he said. 'I want to go to bed.'

'Well, pet, you can stay here if you want to. There's plenty of room.'

'I'm lonely.'

'Oh dear,' said Mrs. Fox. 'I'm afraid we can't help you there. But never mind, it'll be all right.'

'Oh blast you,' said Matthew. 'It won't be all right. It never is.'

Charlie mumbled and smiled sadly.

'Speak up, Charlie,' said Mrs. Fox.

'I was just saying, Dolly, that it's all very sad. But then it's always a little sad to be young and lonely. I have every sympathy with our young friend. He's at a very trying period in his life — if I can help him —'

'How can you help him?' said Mrs. Fox rudely.

'Well, I could bring him home to my place, and we could —'

'No.' She was very white beneath the dollops of rouge.

'No,' she said again. She slumped in her chair. There was hardly a sound then in the white-tiled, cream-ceilinged room. Only the sough of the lilacs in the rising breeze: or of someone's tears, for Mrs. Fox had hidden her face.

'Mrs. Fox is distraite,' said Charlie. 'I can't think why.'

She went for him like a tiger.

'No, I'm not "distraite", as you call it. But I've heard people like you talk before. It's time you were off. And you needn't come back in a hurry.'

She trailed off, and her head fell again to the crook of her
arm. She could hear Charlie's chair scraping as he got up,
and the kitchen door banging after him. Then, his car driving
off, and, as it went, the bells again.

'Oh those bells,' she murmured. 'No wonder they get on
poor Dickie's nerves.'

Her hand reached out and slid until it spilt a cup, and the
coffee ran like black blood on the white-scrubbed table.
What am I doing, she thought, and she raised her head and
saw Matthew beside her, very close. She took his hands and
he raised her up, and she let herself be led by him out into the
garden, past the lilac, and across the wet lawn, to the end of
the the garden where the laburnum grew.

'Imagine,' she said, 'Johnny made me a crown of it.'

She sat down on the garden-seat, self-consciously,
chipping at the cracked paint with her fingers.

'God,' she said. 'It's bad to be young, but it's worse to be
old.'

She heard the breaking of branches over her head, and
looking up, saw Matthew twined in the tree, his long legs
dangling, his face very white through the sheets of gold lace.

'Missis,' he called in a high distant voice. 'I'll make you a
crown of laburnum, a lovely golden crown, and you shall be
the Laburnum Queen.' He slithered to the ground, throwing
down sprays from the tree. He turned, rubbing his legs where
he'd barked them, and bowed to her. Then he draped the
sprays about her head and shoulders, until the blossoms got
into her eyes, and she was plucking nervously at the yellow
foam that crested her forehead, and then thinned out to
trickle untidily down her back.

'My Queen,' he said, and laid his head in her lap.

'There now, love,' she said, 'it'll be all right.'

'No,' he said, 'it never will.'

Perhaps he talked again, but she did not listen to him. She
fingered his hair, and cradled his head in the tangle of
blossom that had fallen to her lap. Occasionally she smiled.
Gradually Matthew fell asleep.

When Johnny came into the garden that morning Mrs.
Fox was asleep too. The laburnum sagged about her
shoulders, and she held Matthew tightly in her arms.

An Unsuitable Relationship

According to Mrs. Fallon, a red sky at night was the shepherd's delight. This observation led her on to a monologue about skies, seasons, landscapes, and finally mountains.

'The mountains now,' she was saying to her unlistening son and his two friends, 'look at them mountains, I declare to me God you can't beat the Dublin mountains.' She took a quick look at her cards, threw one down, her milk-pudding face childish with daring, and continued, 'I remember a ride up the mountains on the back of Larry, God rest him's motor-bike, and there was a red sky, and when we stopped to look back, there was the lights shinin' down below in Dublin, and the sky was black all of a sudden. It put the heart crossways in me.'

She had not drawn the curtains, and if they had wished, the three young men could have seen through the window the broad strip of ground where Mrs. Fallon grew pocked cabbage and limp sweet-pea, and beyond that the fields, dusked as far as the black foothills and the shepherd's delight. But they seemed deep in their 'Newmarket, (chosen because Mrs. Fallon hadn't a 'head' for cards), and besides all three had long since ceased to care about 'the world of nature'. (Wordsworth now, he wrote about 'the world of nature' as distinct from Shelley who was 'an ineffectual bird' and Keats who was a 'lover of beauty'.)

Martin Donnelly, his head fogged from an afternoon's beering in the country, was thinking that Dickie McCarthy and himself should have had more sense than to break their journey back into town. He was aware, dimly, that it is unwise to re-visit glimpses — of the moon, was it? Yet nothing had changed in the Fallon living-room. There was the same special smell, a distillation of stale tobacco and the sweet-pea jammed tight in the glass vase before Our Lady and the lurking steams of greens and char of roast beef. There was the same hand of 'Newmarket' and the same chronic inability of Mrs. Fallon to keep her mind on her cards.

'I'd love a good orange,' she announced.

'Ah will you get on with the game.'

Her son, Peader, she was fond of saying, was a good lad, but a bit hasty.

'Four of clubs wanted,' said Dickie McCarthy.

'The hard Dickie,' said Peadar absently.

It began to rain.

'The room's like a bloody oven,' said Peadar.

'Now,' said Mrs. Fallon firmly. 'Language. You know I don't like —'

'Get on with the bloody game,' her son cut in.

He sucked his teeth. The rain crooned against the window. There were soft wet sounds when the cards flopped against the plastic table-cloth.

'I'd give anything,' said Mrs. Fallon, 'for a good juicy orange.'

'Maybe it's a banana you'd like,' said her son viciously.

'I'm terribly thirsty,' she said. 'Why didn't I bring some in when I was in town!'

'What I'd like,' said Dickie McCarthy, 'is a nice glass of hot rum. I feel cold.'

'Sacred Heart to-night, Dickie McCarthy,' said Peadar, parodying his mother, 'what's the matter with you? It's a terrible warm night.'

'Still, I'd love a jar.'

'Oh be the boys, Dickie,' said Mrs. Fallon, 'you're becomin' a rare one for the drink.' The boldness of her statement flustered her. She pushed back leaky ginger hair from her skim-white cheeks and wetted the tips of her fingers as she sorted her cards.

'What does your mother say about the drink, Dickie?' she asked.

'Oh she doesn't give a damn.'

'Thank God Peadar there doesn't drink much. It's a curse.'

'It's the only pleasure I've left in life,' said Dickie melo-dramatically. And he winked foolishly at Martin. 'There's some I know ...'

'Is it a mot Martin has?' said Peadar. His smoked eyes shone in tip-and-tig flirtation with lustful thoughts.

Martin was pasty.

'The hard Martin,' roared Peadar. 'You were always the eccentric genius.'

'He's an eejut,' said Dickie flatly. ' "Fill high the bowl with Samian wine" is my motto.'

'What's "Samian"?' asked Mrs. Fallon.

'God, you're a great man for the poets,' said Peadar.

'Poetry is all right,' said Mrs. Fallon, 'but some of them men led very bad lives.'

'I suppose next you'll be seein' Christ walkin' on the Liffey.' And Peadar's bray deafened Martin to tears that he blinked back like a cuffed child.

'It's Martin'll be doin' that,' said Dickie triumphantly. 'I'll stick to me pint.'

'All them geniuses has kinks,' said Mrs. Fallon happily.

'Look at Byron,' said Peadar.

'A great man,' said Dickie.

'Look at Oscar Wilde,' said Peadar, 'he was a right boyo.'

'He put himself outside the pale-of-civilisation,' said Mrs. Fallon.

'Him and his green carnation,' said Peadar.

'Them sweet-pea is comin' on grand,' said Mrs. Fallon. 'Will you get on with the bloody game?'

'Anyway,' said Mrs. Fallon, 'how could Martin there see Our Divine Lord on the Liffey? Visions like that are reserved for the Saints.'

'They say he was a man of brilliant intellect,' said Dickie.

'Do you mean Our Lord?'

'No, he doesn't mean Our Lord,' said Peadar savagely, 'he means Oscar Wilde.'

She began to whimper.

'What's up now?'

'That's a terrible thing to say.'

'What?'

'That Our Divine Lord wasn't a man-of-brilliant-intellect.'

'Ah for God's sake.'

Martin stood up.

'Sacred Heart to-night,' said Mrs. Fallon, the milk-pudding wrinkled into a curdle of hospitality.

'Are you off?'

'Yes, we're off,' said Dickie.

'Tell me, Martin, is it true about the mot?' Peadar glittered.

'Yes,' said Martin.

'Go on now, you're joking.'

'I'm in love,' said Martin.

'Glory be to God,' said Mrs. Fallon.

.   .   .   .

There might have been a waterfall close by so great was the din in the trees. There was a faint scent of hay and the air was still moist after the rain.

'We may as well walk it,' said Dickie, 'it's early yet.'

'Yes it's early.'

They walked on sturdily, like two fine young fellows who'd been up the mountains. They returned the salute of a drunk local. They saluted a priest who gave them a fatherly smile.

'That was a bit of a shambles,' said Dickie.

'You must have been still drunk.'

'I'm sorry.'

'Thelma's not a mot.'

'I said I'm sorry.'

'Shut up and walk.'

Never let them know a thing, a single bloody thing. Best keep everything to yourself. Don't wear your heart on your sleeve. No services free in the wound-licking department.

But Dickie wasn't the worst of them. He blundered and
leered, but he meant well. But they were bastards in the digs.
Bastards afraid to go out and get a girl for themselves. The
most they did was have a squeeze at the pictures and
imagine the rest when they got home. They'd never know
what it was like to have a girl like Thelma.

Thelma. Often he went to her place on Sunday nights.
She'd make a spaghetti and curries and stuff, things they
never got in the digs. And there'd be a bottle of wine, maybe
two bottles, and next morning he'd go to the office feeling as
if his body had been washed in olive oil, and during the day
his nostrils would tremor with remembered excitements.
And the celebates knew the signs. Some snickered, some
were snooty. The unknown illicit female unknowingly came
between decent men and their ledgers, pried on them in the
wash-up, scattered their proper routine of horse-talk and
lavatory-joke, and Martin burgeoned in guilt because he
knew that he carried the print of her. His thin neck throbbed
with her love-pulse; when he said 'yes' or 'no' he heard her
huskiness, and when he moved, her unashamed shadow
flitted with him. I am possessed, he thought, and these men
know it.

Dickie knew. Once when Thelma had failed to turn up,
he'd got drunk, and that night he'd babbled out everything to
Dickie in the bed across the room. He talked about her as if
she were the gentlest and loveliest creature in the world, and
when he finished he was talking about her as if she were
a whore. So that Dickie should understand, he'd used the
short filthy words which were common enough in pub-talk,
though drained of carnal meaning. Dickie listened gravely,
and occasionally his mouth pitted, and he shook his head
and said, 'God, Martin, you're goin' the pace.'

They had reached a café with a mottled card announcing
'Hot Soup' in the window.

'We'll have a bowl of soup,' said Dickie.

In the old days before Thelma, they'd always finished up a
night's drinking with a bowl of soup. Sitting over the onion-
flavoured soup, crumbling the fingers of stale bread, watched
by the standard lager-haired waitress, Martin began to feel

warmer towards his blundering potato-faced friend. There was no guile in him, no censure, only an imagination which could not go beyond the dirty words, the sound of them, and the sight of them on untiled walls.

'God,' said Dickie, 'that old Fallon one's an awful bore.'

'Peadar's worse.'

'Fellows change,' said Dickie, 'when they get jobs.'

'Phyllis,' a voice screeched from the kitchen.

'Fill us up another one,' said Dickie. The hearty mood was taking over again. 'Fellas,' said the waitress, and smirked.

They left the money on the table and went out into a silver night. The lamps were lit but they were needless and raw, and already their sad trivial authority had been toppled by the moon.

On the bridge, they stopped to watch a miracle. Along the cabbage-water of the canal a swan glided more luminous than snow in the silver light.

'God,' said Dickie, 'isn't she a beauty.'

Martin Donnelly, clerk of Dublin, lover and mortal sinner, leaned on the cold stone and wept. His friend, who was not the worst, tapped him on the shoulder.

'Forget her,' he said.

Miss Scott

From the steeple in the tenuous air the clock said five to one.

'I didn't think it was that late,' said Miss Scott. Her eyes were cold and large. Miss Scott spoke incisively.

'Didn't you hear the clock strike a quarter-to-one about ten minutes ago?' said Mrs. O'Byrne. Her eyes were friendly and screwed up. Mrs. O'Byrne spoke gently, vaguely; she spoke with a quality of summer in her voice.

Miss Scott and Mrs. O'Byrne were standing in the entrance-porch of the Public Library, where the air was a little warmer than outside on the pavement. Outside on the pavement the air was sharp, it came close to the bone, and coming, stung the flesh.

'That was an unnecessary statement,' said Miss Scott, extra incisively.

'Why?' said Mrs. O'Byrne.

'Because it is now five-to-one — as a matter of fact, it is four minutes to one — it was obviously a quarter to one ten minutes ago.'

'Yes, of course, and what books did you get?'

Miss Scott had a novel by Frances Parkinson Keyes and *The Brontës of Haworth Parsonage,* by Isabel C. Clarke.

'And yours?'

Mrs. O'Byrne had a detective story and the reminiscences of a judge or a barrister or an actor or a cabinet minister or a bishop. 'I don't know exactly what it is,' she said. Miss Scott did not approve of people getting books without knowing exactly what they were about. She did not voice her disapproval, but Mrs. O'Byrne knew what she felt, and touched Miss Scott gently on the elbow.

'We'd better be getting on, hadn't we?'.

Mrs. O'Byrne was a widow and religious. Miss Scott was a convert to the Church and was known to be even more religious than Mrs. O'Byrne. They went together to evening Devotions and Miss Scott would prod Mrs. O'Byrne whenever she noticed in her a tendency to drop off at her Rosary. Mrs. O'Byrne was religious, but frequently had a tendency to drop off not only at her Rosary, but at Mass. When they came out of the Church, Mrs. O'Byrne would excuse herself to Miss Scott and always her voice was gentle and vague and had in it a quality of summer. Miss Scott would not scold Mrs. O'Byrne. Miss Scott spoke incisively and was snappish about mis-statement or unnecessary statement, but never did she scold Mrs. O'Byrne.

Miss Scott walked in the gay bright cold sunshine and half in shadow walked Mrs. O'Byrne. They passed by houses which had beds of gay bright yellow daffodils in their gardens, and in one of the gardens there was a pear-tree in off-white flower. On the pavement there was a small boy whose stockings hung down and who had a long, cruel scratch on his left cheek, and he was looking up at the pear-tree. Miss Scott and Mrs. O'Byrne walked past the church where they had attended all the services and in the garden of the priests' house there were more gay, bright yellow daffodils, and here the sunshine was a little less cold and Mrs. O'Byrne screwed up more her friendly eyes and said that Lent would soon be at an end and they could resume their weekly visits to the pictures. Now Lent would soon be at an end, agreed Miss Scott, and they could look forward to Easter. Mrs. O'Byrne would go away to her cousins in the country on Holy Saturday and, for a week, look at running water and still water, at tall trees and small weak trees, and at many green fields, she said to Miss Scott. Her cousins had sows and horses and pigs and a large dog, a collie she thought it was, but she could not be sure.

Miss Scott did not approve of people being unsure about the breed of dogs, especially when the dogs belonged to close relatives, but she did not voice her disapproval. Never would she scold Mrs. O'Byrne.

Now Lent would soon be over and Miss Scott would be taking up a job at Easter. Miss Scott would superintend seven girls in an office. The girls would be unruly and lazy and cheeky, and, like all girls, even when they are not unruly and lazy and cheeky, over-given to laughing, laughing from nine to five, as if there were anything to laugh about. But Miss Scott would know how to handle them. Miss Scott would never scold Mrs. O'Byrne but, if necessary, she would scold the seven girls who would, if uncurbed, be laughing from nine to five.

Miss Scott and Mrs. O'Byrne put up their umbrellas. The rain fell on a large black mannish umbrella which almost hid Mrs. O'Byrne, and on a small blue dinky umbrella which just did for Miss Scott. The rain was soft and silent, the kind that makes the roads skiddy, it made no sound as it fell on the two umbrellas, no sound at all, said Miss Scott to Mrs. O'Byrne.

'Look at that crowd standing in the rain,' said Mrs. O'Byrne.

'It's not a crowd, merely a small group,' said Miss Scott.

Further up the road there was, indeed, a small group and they seemed careless of the soft, silent rain as they stood by a taxi which was drawn up at the side of the road. The houses now had not, any longer, beds of gay, bright yellow daffodils in their gardens, though one had three single, infinitely slender, yellow daffodils growing in a window-box.

Miss Scott was a curious woman, and although Mrs. O'Byrne tried to pull her back, she pushed her way through the group, which stood careless of the soft, silent rain; pushed her way right to the taxi, and Mrs. O'Byrne called at her gently, 'Miss Scott, Miss Scott.' But Miss Scott had poked her head into the back of the taxi and the soiled red feather on her little blue hat was caught in the window-frame, and behind her she held still open, the small blue dinky umbrella, so that when the policeman came it got in his way. He had to turn Miss Scott around by sheer force and he was very angry with her, very, very angry, but it did not seem to worry Miss Scott. She pushed her way back to Mrs. O'Byrne and Mrs. O'Byrne took her arm. The soft silent rain ceased to fall and the gay, bright, cold sunshine came out again, and now Miss Scott was half in shadow and Mrs. O'Byrne walked in the sunshine: little puff-balls of cloud, smoke-grey cloud, and blue-veined white cloud, skeltered across the sky, the sky gleaming dully with the gay, bright, cold sunshine. The wet road gleamed dully back and the great black and the small blue umbrellas dripped moisture on the pavement, and Mrs. O'Byrne, a gentle, vague woman, wondered that Miss Scott did not speak.

Miss Scott did speak.

'The blood,' she said.

'What blood, dear? Was there blood in the taxi?'

'The blood, the blood,' said Miss Scott.

'Don't think about it any more, dear; it's better to try and forget it.'

'The blood, the blood, the blood,' said Miss Scott.

'Well, tell me about it dear, if you want to, and then try to forget it. Perhaps you'll feel better when you've told me,' said Mrs. O'Byrne.

'There was only blood,' said Miss Scott, 'and a man.'

Miss Scott did not speak incisively. She looked young, like a good young girl who would laugh from nine to five, even if there were nothing to laugh about. Her pale blonde hair gleamed sweetly under her little blue hat with the limp-soiled red feather, the tight skin about her cheekbones was tender and she looked young, said Mrs. O'Byrne, young like a girl; but her eyes were still cold and large, which Mrs. O'Byrne did not say, and also they were fearful, which might have worried Mrs. O'Byrne were it not that she was a gentle, vague woman.

But, yet, she was a little worried. She said it must have been an accident of some kind, must it not, and she hoped that the man was ready to meet his God, who, anyway, was infinitely merciful, and she herself would like to die when the gay, bright yellow daffodils were in the gardens, but not with blood; no, and, of course, she would even more like to die in sight of running water and the still water, the great trees and the small weak trees, and the many green fields.

Where Mrs. O'Byrne's cousins lived, the running water
was a thin, silver curve in the distance, and the still water
was a silver blob. In between were the many green fields.

'God rest his soul,' said Mrs. O'Byrne.

'Happy is the soul the rain falls on,' said Miss Scott, and
still she looked young, like a good young girl.

'Come home with me, dear, and have lunch,' said Mrs.
O'Byrne. 'I have a nice piece of smoked haddock that will do
for both of us, and some nice mashed potatoes, and when we
get home I'll make you a good strong cup of tea, and you'll
feel much better.'

Mrs. O'Byrne and Miss Scott both walked in sunshine
until they reached the little pink-brick house where Mrs.
O'Byrne lived. Mrs. O'Byrne would have liked daffodils in
her garden, but being a vague, gentle woman, did not
bother to have what she wanted and so there were only some
wallflowers which were half in tawny blossom. In the little
untidy living-room of Mrs. O'Byrne's pink-brick house Miss
Scott drank good strong tea and looked more like Miss Scott
and less like a good young girl who might be laughing from
nine to five, if a firm stand were not taken by her superiors.
Mrs. O'Byrne made lunch and said: 'I wonder what
happened? Was he still alive?' and prayed once again
that his poor soul would find peace in the arms of God and
His Blessed Mother. The soft, silent rain came down again
and gentle, vague women could not know what Miss Scott
was thinking. Gentle, vague women would never think of the
soft, silent rain falling on a man drained of all his blood,
falling on him through his wooden box as they laid him in the
clay of spring, while his people wept and the yellow daffodils
were not gay or bright, and through the spangled, wet air his
soul passed to the arms of the infinitely merciful God, whom
Miss Scott had embraced but a little while ago. A little while
ago she told Mrs. O'Byrne when first she met her at a Sale of
Work stall. The gentle, vague woman made lunch and was
dimly anxious about Miss Scott, who drank good strong tea,
and now looked quite like Miss Scott, and not at all like a
young girl with the skin tender at the cheek-bones and a sad
sweet gleam in her pale blonde hair.

Jewman

Myer was dying. In a morphine dream he muzzled ponies, and from a giraffe Rabbi Rubinstein wagged a long spiky finger of grimed ivory. A nurse, fair-skinned, blonde-haried, a Viking throw-back, sat by his bed and watched his bitten lower lip rise to, and fall from, the nicotined upper. There were white cotton roses on his bedspread and white faintly sumptuous screens closed Myer and his guardian off from the other three occupants of the room. They had all seen death before. They had seen between them the death of a young wife, the death of an old mother, and the death of a little brother. They had seen the deaths of Christians, fortified by the rites of Holy Church, entering the familiar kindom of night with assurance and even joy.

The little brother. Padge was lucid before his last suspension of breath, Ignatius remembered, and he talked happily to the whole family, daddy and mammy and Maureen and Lily and Ignatius himself. He died, thought Ignatius, like a little saint. And that's what he was now in Heaven, Ignatius decided, a young angel watching over them all and praying for them all. Ignatius wandered off among baby trumpets and white lace.

Myer moaned. The Viking nurse wiped away the hoar of sweat from his forehead, straightened the turned-down sheets, white except for a little fawn tea-stain.

The old mother had made a good death, thought John the Punter. There were many Johns in this section of the hospital, and the old-established patients had special

designations. John the Punter specialized in 'doubles' and
'trebles' and was reported to have winners daily. But he was
now taking time off from studying form for next day and he
remembered the clutter of old ones in his mother's bedroom
and the faint smell of whiskey from the priest's breath and
the last, long, shining look from his mother's mahogany eyes
and he felt again the satisfaction of reasonable grief, the
sense of duty done, of social fulfilment. He had stood by the
mother till the end and ever after he would pass for a good
son. Only like a misremembered dream, then and now, an
image of a young hurt childish face touched his
consciousness, touched and dissolved and good riddance.
Kitty Hagerty was now blown up like a harvest frog, a slut
with a brood of sickly sharp-voiced little devils. The mother
smiled at John the Punter, and John the Punter knew that the
mother had been right. He said a Hail Mary quickly for the
happy repose of her soul. It was time to get up and make a
cup of tea.

Joseph was not thinking of the young wife. He had long
ago stopped thinking about the scraggy bride of three
months. But as he lay with his ears cocked for the rhythms
of Myer's breathing, as he weighed his chances of assisting
at the death of a Jew, surely an awful and fierce occasion, he
did pause to thank God that all belonging to him had died a
holy and a happy death and in his review of a blessed tribe
Mary Quinn had a distant smudged place. Joseph did not
know why it was that the girl he had courted and married
was less actual to him than St. Jude or St. Anthony or St.
Martin, he did not even think that it was odd.

John the Punter was making for the door stealthily. He
looked up and down the corridor, listened, and decided the
kitchen was empty. Joseph watched him hungrily, and as
soon as John the Punter had gone, he swung out of bed and
put on his dressing gown. It was a great checked dressing
gown and its enormous collar shrunk his round smooth-
topped head until it seemed like a ball balanced on a hillock
of cloth. Only his famished eyes, brilliant as a blue-bag,
livened a head that invited flips of the finger.

As soon as Joseph was out of the door, Ignatius sat up

and combed his hair. He made a cindery quiff with the help
of a pocket mirror his mother had given him, smiled at his
bockety reflection, but not through vanity, for he knew that a
truly pious man must not be vain of his physical appearance.
He smiled because he thought his face was funny, all sharp
angles and bony sallies, like a cartoon of a thin man in the
paper. The holy comedian skipped to the door, into the
glooming corridor where Our Lady watched in an aureole of
fairy-lights. Joseph was just turning into the kitchen after
John the Punter when Ignatius bobbed ceremoniously to Our
Lady.

The kitchen was ample, gleaming, hot as hell on a summer
evening. The windows opened to shorn fields where cats with
the backs of greyhounds limbered from clump to clump of
docken. Cut grass in heaps was bleaching to sand. A spire,
cross-topped, barely showed through the soughing woods.
By the electric stove John the Punter straddled with an
aluminium teapot and his narrow rust-flecked jaws were
quivering.

'Are you making a cup of tea?' said Joseph, compelling
with his blue-bags.

'Don't you know bloody well I'm making a cup of tea?
Don't you come in here every night snooping and scrounging
and snarling?'

'Language, John, language. I come from a home where I
never heard such language.'

'John and Joseph must agree,' called Ignatius. There was
a remote, clear chirrup from unseen birds.

'And I suppose you want tea too,' said John the Punter.
'I'm telling you there'll be trouble here some night.'

'Ah John dear, you've the heart of gold beneath it all.'

'If I have,' said John the Punter, 'there won't be much of it
left by the time you boyos are finished nibbling at my
generosity.'

'I'd die only for the cup of tea before settlin' down to my
prayers,' said Joseph.

'There's great heart in a nice cup of tea at bed-time,' said
Ignatius.

'Why don't you make it yourself? Why do you have to

come bobbing in here after me, night after night, week after week, year after ...' He stopped and muttered on to himself and Joseph's eyes revolved, intense beacons, and the overheated kitchen clamoured silence.

But Ignatius said happily, 'Three year come July.'

'Bring over your cup,' said John the Punter, and he scooped the rustling tea into the pot and clamped the caddy noisily. In or about that time Myer began the journey that did or did not end in Abraham's bosom. The Viking nurse knew what she had to do, and another nurse, bunty, cherry cheeked, bustling, came at the ring of a bell, and soon two little men in soiled blue serge and battered hats came to watch over the chrysalis.

In the kitchen there was turbulence. The cherry-cheeked nurse had run down the missing patients. She blazed at them. John the Punter remembered the furies of the mother, Ignatius thought of the little brother caught stealing raisins got in for the making of the Christmas pudding and tried to look like him, Joseph thought of the trials of the saints. 'You bitch,' he repeated under his breath, 'you bitch, you bitch.'

She flayed them, finishing up with, 'And poor old Myer dead down there, and you fellows kicking up murder in the kitchen. Suppose a doctor come in here, or the Night Sister, or Assistant Matron, or Matron?'

'So Myer's dead,' said John the Punter. 'Mind you he wasn't bad for a Jewman.'

'God rest his soul,' said Ignatius.

'There's no salvation outside the Church,' said Joseph.

'God is merciful,' said Ignatius. The little brother had once come home and said a Jewman had given him sixpence for lighting the gas.

'You've a bitter tongue, Joseph,' said John the Punter.

'I don't believe that,' said the cherry-cheeked nurse. The cherries were lambent.

'Maybe we should say a prayer for him,' said Ignatius.

'He had a good eye for the horses,' said John the Punter.

'He was a kind old man,' said the nurse.

'There's no salvation —' began Joseph.

'Christ Almighty, how do you know that?' roared John

the Punter.

'Joseph and John,' said Ignatius.

'Get back to your beds this minute,' said the nurse.

'Outside the Church,' said Joseph.

'Damn the Church,' moaned John the Punter. 'It's the Man Above that has the say.'

'That's blasphemy,' said Joseph.

'Sure he didn't mean it,' said Ignatius.

'I'll give you five minutes, and if you're not out of here when I come back, I'll ring the Assistant Matron.'

And she bustled off with anger and fear in her heart, for Myer was a good old man and yet Joseph might be right.

'Some night, I'm telling you, there'll be a hanging here,' said John the Punter.

'She means well,' said Ignatius.

She's a bitch, thought Joseph. Anyone was a bitch who'd prevent a sick man having three or four cups of tea in comfort.

There was a dull rose light behind the trees. One premature star signalled. John the Punter's narrow jaws looked purple in the dusk. He sluiced the teapot, scalded the cups, wiped up bubbles of tea on the stove's edge. Ignatius gave a little jig, and then remembered himself.

'Myer's better off,' he said.

'Let's hope so,' said John the Punter.

'He was a Jewman,' said Joseph.

'Sure wasn't Our Lord a Jewman?' said Ignatius.

'He became a Christian,' said Joseph.

'God give me patience,' said John the Punter.

Suddenly Joseph moved steadily to the door. He went out to the middle of the corridor, turned in the direction of the lavatories.

'I seen it,' he said.

'You seen what?' said John the Punter.

'There's no salvation outside the Church.'

'And where did you see it?'

'I seen it in a holy book ' And he moved swiftly away towards the lavatories.

That second John the Punter and Ignatius heard the tap-

tap, like a blindman's stick, of the Assistant Matron.
Judgment was upon them while Joseph lowered himself
happily onto the bowl.

Honeymoon

I

'Thank God,' said Laura to Jo-Jo who had come to her side to stand there like a famished madonna. 'Lottie's tight and father's tight and if we stay any longer Tony and I will be tight and we'll miss the plane.'

Jo-Jo leaned down to Laura's upturned head and kissed her. A little after Laura went to her room to change, and her father, maudlin by this time, slobbered a little on Jo-Jo's shoulder. But she had alchemized her grief into fury at some as yet undefined person or object, and Laura's father found no comfort.

As Laura came to the staircase, Jo-Jo went to her again and spoke to her. Her body loped and strained in her long black dress, and Laura's face was shadowed when she came down into the hall. It was time to go.

Laura and Tony were to be driven alone to the airport, where they were to be flown straight to Paris. Everybody was agreed that the wedding-breakfast was a great success. 'A credit to poor Auntie Jo-Jo,' as Laura's father had said. Jo-Jo had shown untypical tact and ingenuity in pairing off guests. For Laura the crown of Jo-Jo's achievement had been the coupling-off of Herbert and Lottie, two survivals from Tony's and Laura's college days. Herbert was a Gold Coast negro who had studied Medicine in Tony's time, and Lottie had been an extravagantly unsuccessful student of Modern Languages while Laura was distinguishing herself.

By dint of regular and voluminous correspondence, they had succeeded in becoming part of the bric-à-brac in Tony's and Laura's lives.

'I can't imagine how we came to know them at all,' said Laura. 'But there they are, and we'll have to put up with them.'

All through the breakfast she had shot dazzling glances at Herbert and Lottie, and under this battery of radiance, the two felt themselves united in a conspiracy of adoration, and became friendly. Jo-Jo winked at Laura, and Laura winked at Tony and the drink flowed.

Lottie had asked for the salt in a mortified voice.

'You like salt, Miss Carstairs?' asked Herbert.

'Oh yes — may I call you Herbert? All my family are partial to salt. During the war, when we were living in Richmond, my mother used to have quite a thing about wasting salt. She used to hoard it, but unfortunately we discovered too late that the cupboard was damp. My mother was simply furious.'

'You are partial to condiments in general, Miss Carstairs?' asked Herbert, who did not ask might he call her 'Lottie'.

'Oh no, indeed,' replied Lottie. 'All my family are on the whole averse to condiments.' She was warming up.

'Except of course for salt — ever since my poor mother took ill after a week in Paris on those nasty French foods. The French, in *my* opinion, go in for an excessive use of condiments. My mother came out all over in spots, nasty red things they were. Ever since then we have preferred to eat with great simplicity — though of course we have our little fads. No, we like good plain fare. Plain — but good.'

Lottie's glass was refilled and Herbert grew bolder.

'You seem to be a very united family, Miss Carstairs.'

'Oh yes, we are indeed. Which is not to say that we are not individualistic as individuals — I mean — Oh dear, can one say that?'

But Laura's most vivid memory of her wedding was to be of her last sight of her friends and relations grouped in the doorway, or hanging from windows in snowy white-lace-curtains topped by fawn blinds, or scurrying to the gate with slack mouths and champagne-aerated *Bons Voyages*. She was to remember the two exactly parallel streams of tears running from her father's porched eyes, and many times during the next month she was to see again with tremor of the heart Jo-Jo's lean greyhound body and her immutable Sienese face.

They drove away in a burst of sunlight and through the hurting glare, Laura made an effort to take it all in, to stock-pile for the hungry days some details of the lucent present. Her father and Jo-Jo were her childhood and young girlhood. Lottie, great swollen girl was, if nothing else, a symbol of college days remoter now than the days of her fairy childhood. And there was Tony's Herbert, beaming in ivory at the dash and beauty of this couple who were his friends, and high in the house, very near the sky it seemed, three female cousins from God knows where, with long red hair hanging down their backs and voices like sea-birds, sang out 'I know my love' in clear gold August post-noon air.

Laura lay back in Tony's tobaccoed tweeds and was content to hold in her mind the light-stippled moments of her so successful wedding breakfast.

II

'Darling Aunt Jo-Jo,' she wrote, 'I feel a bit lonely sitting here without Tony who's gone to the café. I wonder sometimes if it's wise to be so dependent on another human being. You'll think I'm daft but without him I feel like I'd suddenly gone blind or lost my sense of touch.'

She managed to finish her letter before half-past ten. She fixed her make-up, threw on a light coat about her shoulders, and consciously throwing her head high, made down the Boulevard St. Germain. The breeze was stirring up, played in her hair, and she threw her head higher still. She might have been of the *ancien régime*. Some yards ahead her guillotine lay ready. The stars were cold in the navy-blue night.

At first she could not see Tony. Sara and Helen, two

American divorcées, were alone at a table. Tony's usual
cronies were getting on well without him. And then she saw
him. He sat, away from the others, with a stranger, a young
man of twenty or so. He had his glass raised, and he was
smiling and he looked up happily at the cold stars. He saw
Laura, and he waved. Her heart began to pound, she ran
through the tables, and came panting to Tony's table. She
felt a tiny bubble of sweat on her left nostril.

'Sit down, darling,' said Tony. He did not get up, but the
stranger did. 'This is a — Danish friend, Mr. Holger
Bjornson. Mr. Bjornson doesn't speak English very well, but
we're getting along nicely in German.'

'Hello,' she said simply. She had a ludicrous temptation to
cry out plaintively, 'But darling, you *know* I did French and
Italian.' She bit her lip, and drank rapidly the cognac Tony
had ordered. 'Jibber-jabber, jibber-jabber' she thought
unjustly as she watched the Dane. She knew a little German,
but clearly Tony was nor concerned with keeping the
conversation on her level. Soon she found herself smiling at
jokes she didn't understand, and the smiles, she felt, did not
always come in the right places. God, she thought, Tony's
being damn rude to me. Yet he smiled continually and
seemed unaware of any awkwardness. He burst into laughter
at something the Dane said, and Laura asked curtly, 'Would
you mind translating, please?'

She realised that he was drunk. His eyes glittered. His lips,
always full, seemed to have thickened. But she was not
prepared for what he said.

'Holger thinks it would be a good thing if you left us.'

Once said, it seemed inevitable. The knocking in her heart
seemed familiar. Tony was still smiling. Holger looked at her
curiously. It was a moment scooped out of time and place.

She got up. The Dane is very beautiful, she thought.

'You are go-ing, old girl?' he said in English.

'Yes,' she said, 'my husband will explain.' Even while she
said it, she was ashamed of the stress she laid on the word
'husband'. She turned and walked over to Sara and Helen.
The table was littered with charge-slips. They too had drunk
well to-night.

'I saw honey,' said Sara. *'Garçon, trois gins à l'eau.'*
The waiter came. When he had gone, Sara spoke.
'I saw honey, I saw. Drink your gin, honey.'
'Yes honey,' said Helen, 'drink your gin.'
Laura gulped her drink.
'It doesn't matter, honey,' said Sara, 'I've seen this kind of
thing before.'
'What kind of thing?' she answered stupidly.
'Young princes,' said Sara. 'They come along and they're
poison. I've seen it happen to the most ordinary decent men.'
The gin was working on top of the cognac. She wanted,
absurdly, to sing. She thought of the three mad, red-haired
cousins, flown with champagne, singing from the billowing
white curtains, 'I know my love . . .' There had been a young
prince in college, in her French class. All the girls, and
perhaps some of the boys had been in love with him. The
Prince of Denmark *à la tour abolie.* She began to cry, a
childish, undignified sniffle.
Helen gave her a handkerchief. They had many more gins.
Boys and girls walked down the pavement arm-in-arm. In the
silver shadow of the Church of St. Germain a couple
embraced for minutes. Drunken American yells klaxoned
over the buzz of the café. Out of the corner of her eye, Laura
saw Tony and the Dane. Good-night, sweet prince. *Puisque
je retrouve un ami si fidèle . . .*
'Encore trois gins à l'eau,' said Sara. Laura drank
wept. The two women gave her handkerchiefs and told her to
drink up. Sara had a wild look in her eyes, but remained
placid. Helen breathed fast. It was one o'clock.
'Listen, honey,' said Sara gently, 'crying your eyes out
won't do you any good. He'll probably come back to you.
Most of them do. I was one of the unlucky ones.'
'He'll never come back,' she said.
'May I have the key, darling?' Tony was beside her. He
swayed slightly.
'Why?'
'Oh, nothing. I just thought I'd turn in. And I promised
Holger a night-cap.'
'Go to hell,' she said.

He lurched back to his table.

'Give him the key,' said Sara.

'No, I can't. I can't stand it.'

'Give it to him and see what happens.'

She would give it to him. She walked across to them, trying hard to stay erect and aloof. She laid the key on the table. But he hardly looked at it. Only the Dane looked at her with great spaniel eyes. As she walked back to Sara and Helen, she began to pray. Dear Mother, let him not leave me. Sacred Heart, let him come back to me. Saint Anthony, please help me. God please, please. Sacred Heart of Jesus, I put my trust in Thee.

'I had it for three years before he left me,' said Sara. To Laura's horror, Sara had begun to cry, soundlessly and motionlessly, like a cow. And Helen was stroking Sara's hand with gentle cooing noises.

'Don't lose him,' said Sara suddenly. 'Go over to him and find him again.'

Laura did not move.

'Damn you, you silly bitch,' bellowed Sara. 'Don't lose him.'

There was a crash, the tinkle of falling glass, a flood of French invective. Tony had fallen from his chair. Laura leaped up and ran across to the little crowd that had gathered. He lay sheet-white and helpless while the Dane was tugging at his arm. Together they picked him up, a dead weight splayed between their sagging arms.

'Come along, darling,' she whispered. 'Come along.'

They propped him across to the taxi-rank. The driver they found looked at her, pityingly. *'Trop bu,'* he muttered, *'trop bu, comme tous les Américains.'*

The Dane was furious. *'Il n'est pas Américain.* He is a descendant of kings.'

The Dane helped her to undress him. Tony muttered balderdash about changing-rooms in his stupor. His romantically sad lips contorted and spat. His film-star forehead was dripping. They could not manage to button his pyjama jacket or tie the string of his pyjama trousers, and Laura could not turn away her eyes from the black curly hair at the breast and pit of his torso.

'Do you want a drink?'

'Ah no, old girl,' said the Dane. 'But smile, you smile nicely, old girl.'

'I'm hardly in the humour for smiling.' She noticed that his skin was as fresh as a girl's. She leant forward and kissed him on the lips. Then she let him out. They had not spoken again. Towards dawn Tony dragged her into his arms.

Two days later, they left for Dublin.

Misadventure

Three very thin persons, two men and a woman, were sitting
on the stone balustrade by the lake. As they were very thin
and had forgotten to bring cushions from one of the
salons in the Castle, they were continually wriggling and
shunting. It had not occurred to them that the Castle was
only a few yards away, and that it would be sensible to fetch
cushions, and so enjoy in comfort the soft warm air and the
silence and the olive and lavender mountain across the lake.
In true daylight the mountain was blue and not very
interesting. As the light died, the blue swam and, since the
three very thin persons had been trained to enjoy nature
when it was most like art, they often sat after the weighty
Castle dinner, and watched, while they digested, what the
diminshing light did to the mountain. They forgot always to
bring cushions, and so always, they wriggled and shunted.

Jonathan, the eldest of the three, a distinguished
intellectual in his own, unlocated, time, wriggled and shunted
in a circumspect way, not unlike the manner in which his
mind worked. Slattery, his second-in-
command, accompanied his wrigglings with snorts and low
snarling sounds. There was a personal enmity between him
and the balustrade. The youngest of the three, Gretta,
Jonathan's secretary and Slattery's part-time mistress,
wriggled with petulant comments, chief of which was the
observation that it was hell. It would be difficult to say what
she meant by this, since for Gretta hell was an all-embracing
comparison. Life in the Castle, for instance, was hell. But so

too was life outside it, down along the white, dusted road, in the little village it led to, in the remote and yearned-for world beyond the village. And people, in and out of the Castle, were hell: the young sergeant from the Army Base (for the Americans were still in Austria) who got drunk every night and wept about the distant fishing-trips to Alaska, the expansive yellow-haired matron who sold them soap and pencils and cheap slim copy-books, the women in the beergardens who brought them tankards of amber beer and little frail glasses of *schnapps,* all of them, the routine, normal, indestructible people of the world, were hell.

Slattery prided himself on exactitude in thought and speech, and would sometimes take her up on her habit of finding hell wherever she went. 'Hell?' he'd ask, 'what do you mean, hell?' And he would talk about the necessity in our time for definition, for mental clarity, for accuracy. 'Accuracy above all,' he'd say, with a kind of relish similar to that of his cousin, the unemigrated Irish priest, lecturing on Purity to the peasants of Connemara. Slattery, certainly, was accurate. He knew exactly the number of times he had slept with a woman, a particularly striking accomplishment, given his constitutional aversion to continency. He knew how many novels by Simenon he had read, and remembered their titles. He could even remember how many drinks he had had, when last the people of the Castle had gathered in the great hall, and danced together, stiffly, sadly, like clockwork figures drained, in the wash, of colour.

Jonathan now, he too liked figures of speech, but his range was very much wider than Gretta's. His enemies, who were many and of disparate interests, claimed that the making of metaphors was the solitary prolonged activity that went on behind his high off-white forehead. He was at it again this evening.

'It's hell,' said Gretta.

'No Gretta,' he said gently, 'not hell ... perhaps purgatory.'

'What do you mean?' asked Slattery, with inordinate bitterness.

'I mean,' said Jonathan, with a great meaningless gesture,

'that this life of ours is actually the condition of being which
the theologians call Purgatory, that this lake is only a great
ferny bowl to be emptied like — like a chamber-pot — when
the hour of deliverance cometh, and that the willows, those
themselves lamentable symbols of our sadness, will one day
be transmuted into the unimaginable trees of Paradise.'

'Oh my suffering aunt,' said Slattery, 'why the hell should
the lake be emptied?'

'I like the lake,' said Gretta in her ready-to-hand small-girl
voice. 'It's a nice blue lake and I don't want it emptied, and
I'm very glad to be sitting beside it.'

'Attagirl,' said Slattery. The bad winter of his face
brightened a moment, and he gave her a savage pat on the
rump.

The dying light softened the three faces, made them seem
tranquil and innocent, smoothed away here an unsatisfied
lust, there an unsurfaced memory. When Joanthan spoke
again, his companions felt it as they might have felt the
tongue mortifying an open nerve.

'I hate the lake,' said Jonathan, in a strange, natural voice.

Their interrogations came at him like hailstones. And he
fled. In a moment he had swung away up the steps to the
Castle. Oh God, he thought, I've been here too long. I need a
change, I'm no longer able to cope with the young and the
youngish.

'Come back and tell us why,' called Gretta in a high,
budgerigar squeak.

'Come back and tell us why,' called Slattery in a high,
parrot squawk.

Well, they'd done their worst. They had reminded him of
that death. Not that he needed reminding. But somehow this
evening, the memory was more coherent, more solid than
usual. He had better let them know about it. And perhaps,
when he had moved on, they would, with his knowledge, be
able to prevent another such death in the Castle. He came
slowly down the steps.

They seemed too young, this couple the Board had sent
out to assist him. A Ph.D. and a liberal attitude towards sex
were insufficient equipment for the task of safeguarding the

people in the Castle. They must learn that maladies of the spirit existed, more dangerous and less obvious than any physical disorder.

'All right,' he called, 'I'll tell you why I hate the lake.' Suddenly they seemed to him sad and mendicant and he experienced a familiar gush of synthetic tenderness.

'As Dr. Gogarty says,' he proclaimed aloud, ' "Death may be very gentle after all".'

He plunged a hand into his hair, in the manner born of Irish littérateurs encountered during his 'time'. He fingered a non-existent black cravat, and settled himself cautiously to begin. Dead on time, another more sombre light purpled the mountain. He was distracted. 'Nature,' he said, 'how banal she can be. I suppose she thinks she's helping, like a bad stage-electrician.'

'Oh Jonathan,' said Gretta, 'you're hell,' and Slattery snarled disgustedly.

'When I first came to the Castle,' said Jonathan, 'I was full of hope, buoyed up with the expectation of finding a solidity, a permanence, existence which would be really existence, and not merely a series of *moments parfaits* strung on a chain of non-existence . . . Forgive again my metaphor,' he giggled.

'Cut the cackle,' said Slattery viciously. Gretta began to clack her heels.

'You drop, yourself, into metaphor, my dear chap,' said Jonathan. 'Anyway I soon observed that life in the Castle differed only slightly from the old life. The difference was one of degree — one got a little drunker, fell in love just a little more deeply, fell out of love just a little more quickly . . .'

'I said, cut the cackle,' snarled Slattery. Gretta clacked more furiously, like a demented Spanish dancer.

'I'll come to the 'osses,' said Jonathan wearily. 'Yes, indeed, the boy who died probably loved horses. And I suppose some would have called him a splendid young animal.' He was silent, and for once they were patient with him. He seemed so tired, so natural, like an old actor who has taken off his make-up. When he began again, they scarcely recognised the quiet, colourless voice.

'He was called Andrew. He played tennis a lot, swam a
lot, smoked occasionally, drank moderately, and ate heartily.
He was twenty-five. He had, as mistress, incomprehensibly,
a dotty young woman with the brains of a bird.'

Slattery looked aggressive, as if challenged on the
intellectual quality of his own ladies, but relaxed.

'He had one major eccentricity. He adored sacred music.
When in the morning we saw grey rings under his eyes, we
knew that probably he had lain most of the night in the
music-room, listening to Palestrina and Bach and Mozart.
And he loved fishing. Sometimes at day-break he would go
away to the mountains, dressed in a very bulky and quite
preposterous fishing-costume, and return only at dusk, with
a pannier of speckled trout. These he would have fried for his
supper, and he would share them with whoever happened to
be sitting at his table.' Jonathan appeared overcome. Gretta
clacked her heels gently, then again furiously. Slattery
snarled softly. Jonathan recovered. 'So it continued for what,
in retrospect, seems a very long time. But it was no more
than five weeks. Five weeks and we did that to him . . .
Andrew was known and loved by all the people in the Castle.
I remember their bright faces when we invited them to eat
trout or hear Bach. And I remember how radiant, truly
radiant, were the faces of those who came to watch when he
went swimming in the lake. He was all gold, like a god.'

Jonathan's voice was sad and true, so that Gretta, and
Slattery even, looked out over the lake for the young man
who was all gold like a god. Their imaginations failed, and
they wrapped themselves in their own thin freckled limbs.
The cicadas struck up, and Jonathan turned his great bogus
head to the gathering stars.

'When he came ashore, four or five would rush to give him
towels. But Andrew liked to do things for himself . . . And
when he played tennis with Nana, his dotty young woman,
some of us thought that here, perhaps, at last, by the green
court, with the white players and the soft plonk of the tennis
balls, and the silly tender jargon of the game — that here at
last was the good life, and that we had glimpsed the Golden
Age.'

Slattery and Gretta stayed quiet; Jonathan felt again the facile tenderness, but this time accompanied by an impulse towards expression. He would have gathered them in his arms, Gretta meringue-faced and topped with lemon curd, Slattery plum-nosed and frost-sharpened, his straggling foxy hair more unsuccessful than any wig. He stayed the ludicrous gesture and went on.

'We were all so grateful, I think, for this initiation into the good and gentle. We were foolish enough to believe that Andrew was happy with us, with Nana, with the long days watching the trout in the mountains, the long nights stretched on the floor of the music room, while the sacrifice of the Mass was celebrated in art. God knows we ourselves had little to offer beyond our capsules of culture and our liberalism.'

Jonathan plucked at his nose irritably.

'Don't pick your nose,' snapped Slattery, hackles raised by a possibly lurking sneer at the liberal ethic.

'Be quiet,' said Gretta, like a human being.

'It was Nana,' said Jonathan, 'poor vague little Nana, who first noticed that something was wrong, but soon we could all see the change. He waded in so slowly from the lake, and once or twice even, he let himself be towelled. He stopped going to the mountains. Sometimes he would stay all night in the music-room.'

The usual red star took its place, hung out from the sky, over the black mountain. The pine trees were seen again in the lake, whitened in ridges by the moonlight. The night air chilled.

'The second last night I saw him,' said Jonathan, '— but no, it was really morning — I was coming back with some of the kids, from the beergarden. We were all quite high, and we roamed through the Castle, through all our lovely rooms, till we heard the sound of music. And there he was stretched out as usual, Adam clothed and fallen, listening to the St. Matthew Passion. We all backed away, sobered and faintly scandalised.'

Jonathan got up, smoothed his trouser-seat, and turned out to the lake.

'It happened the following morning. I was sitting here as usual, smoking, watching that damned mountain. It was in the morning. I heard a woman's voice shrilling out from under the awning. It was Nana. "It's too cold, Andy darling, don't go, it's too cold." And then I saw Andrew coming down the steps, a towel over his shoulder. She ran after him, pulled at his arm, and somehow his elbow struck hard against her face. She began to whimper, and he gathered her in his arms as a man not caring for domestic animals might comfort a wounded cat. She clung to him, until he had to put her down on the steps, and on he went while she called, "Don't go, Andy darling, it's too cold, too cold".'

Jonathan's voice was stagey again. He could not resist the moment's opportunity, the recital of a death to an eager audience, the moonlight, the sheened lake, the black mountain and its bloody star.

'I should have stopped him,' he howled.

'Why didn't you? rasped Slattery.

'Oh, it was hell,' said Gretta.

'I didn't,' said Jonathan, 'because so seldom one foresees that life can become literature. And so I watched him cleave and plunge through the water, until he was gone. One can go on dreaming while people die. While he died, I thought only of the green court and Nana, and the summer afternoons like a dispensation. It was quite still. There was no call for help, no anguish on the water. And then his white duck-coat slipped from the balustrade, went billowing in the scum, got tangled in the reeds.'

The red star was the colour of a sanctuary lamp. Slattery began to fondle Gretta's waist. Death was real and earnest, but the habitual night lust had dominion. Gretta breathed more heavily. The boy was dead, the story was over, the rest would be Jonathan's maundering guilt.

'And Nana?' rusted Slattery suprisingly.

'She was beside me. She picked up his shoes, took out the carefully folded American tie, kissed it, and said she had told him it was too cold.'

Jonathan swayed theatrically, regained position, and blew his nose.

'They found his body, still gold, but muddied and slimed, at the far side of the lake.'

'The funeral arrangements,' said Slattery hoarsely. 'Was he a Catholic?'

'His papers said he was an Anglican. But I had him laid in the chapel here, and then he was sealed, and his parents came and took him home to England. His mother wore tweeds and sensible shoes, and had waved white hair. She kissed Nana ... His father was an ex-major in the British Army, with a big ginger moustache. He cried when they brought the coffin from the Castle.'

'And Nana?' Slattery asked again.

'We had to send her away. She took to nymphomania and the Board heard about it.'

'It was hell,' said Gretta, and Slattery contented himself with the silent motions, sufficiently grotesque, of imitation.

They went up the steps together, the three very thin people. The red star paled, the moonlight thinned, and somewhere down the road, the Castle's English contingent, flown on beer, sang *Drink to me only*. Gretta and Slattery went to his cold whitewashed room, and made greedy passionless love. Jonathan went to his study, wrote a report, and settled down over a bottle of whiskey and the photos of dead and absent friends. Taut and foamy-lipped, he watched through the night, and saw again the transformed blue mountain. Gretta moaned in her sleep, and dreamed that the tallow-white body beside her was all gold, lichened with the green things of the lake. The earliest leaves were falling on Andrew's grave, and when his parents came in the afternoon, they would pick them from his coverlet of marble chips.

Spring In Beeston Street, Dublin 2

'On the sham-mahogany counter were two porter rings caused by, resulting from, the glasses of the last two drinkers.'

A good hard statement that. Anyone reading that would say to himself: this is no overture to adolescent self-pity, no malcontent whine, but the signature of eyes that see, of a brain that has the impetuous heart to heel.

Mícheál Jenkins, B.A., B.Comm., aged twenty-five and living off his daddy, a retired bank manager in the Midlands, took a gobble at his pint of stout, untangled from his pocket a filthy handkerchief, nonsensically wiped a stout blob from his writing pad, leaned back, and leaned forward again quickly. The chair-backs of Aloysius Counihan had been known to give.

'The hard man,' roared Mr. Counihan, 'anyone'd think you were dead the way you're starin' at me.'

'I beg your pardon, Mr. Counihan.' Jenkins was a very polite young man and his dead mammy had told him it was rude to stare at people.

'Now I'll give you something to stare at. Will you take an eyeful of that?'

Mr. Counihan tore a sheet from a memo pad and grinned bestially. On it were itemized certain rounds of drinks acquired during the week and unpaid for by Jenkins.

'You'll be paid,' said Jenkins. 'Mr. Counihan, you'll be paid.'

'I'm damn sure I will,' said Mr. Counihan.

The swing door grated horribly, and Aloysius ram-rodded to smile, like a man surprised on the lavatory, at Mrs. Layton-Desmond who was coming in looking rather more the worse for wear than usual. Mrs. Layton-Desmond was a very difficult and convivial lady much respected by staff and clients for her lack of side.

'Micheál,' she cried, 'may I join you?'

'Of course. What'll you have?'

'Will you listen to the boy!'

Jenkins finished his pint quickly and ordered two gins and a tonic from Mr. Counihan whose fist was shaking from one eye. There was no point in not having full value from the round-game. Seven years in the bitter and bloody war of Dublin's pubs had exiled shame, though even now it made a cringing attempt at a come-back.

'I'm absolutely *dead*,' said Mrs. Layton-Desmond. Being slightly fuddled Jenkins very naturally put the obvious question.

'When did you die?'

She played the game like the gentry she was.

'Oh roughly — *very* roughly — mind you, about twenty-five years ago.'

'And was it swift and sure, or was it a kind of dissolution?'

'Well in my case it was all over quite quickly.' She managed a little *moue* to signify wry discomfort and went on, 'But I have observed the phenomenon as a gradual process.'

'You are unwilling to give further details.'

'Well I'd rather not. It's such a personal matter.'

She repeated the round in a lovely uncondescending manner, succinct testimony of her absence of side.

Jenkins was looking at his pad. 'On the sham-mahogany counter . . .' (For the death of me, he thought, I don't know what that means.) But all this was real. The draughty bar, the smell of urine and porter, the clattering swing door that led to the morning he'd seen earlier in Spring get-up as he walked through the Green. No question they existed. And in the present. *That was it*. A new kind of hypersensitive minute by minute autobiography larded with gobbets of

flash-back starting now, just now this very moment as he
watched the delicate ruby-tipped claw of Mrs. Layton-
Desmond juggle tonic, tenderly acrid, into her juniper juice
... ah that autumn Sunday beyond Templeogue picking
blackberries, fingers inked with juice, a large round sweet tin
full of glistening, downed, panelled fruit and first love and
first lust for Carmel's little dairies, ah Jesus the flash-back's
going on too long. Anyway the whole thing could be faked
and would warrant the remove to London. . . .

   'I wish you'd answer my question, dear boy. For the third
time, have you finished your book yet?'
   'What book?'
   'The book you're writing, sillyums.'
   'I'm not writing any bloody book,' said Jenkins with
passion.
   No. This was it. No flash-backs. No sheen of the
blackberry. No sour-acid-sweet breath and no Carmel, with
or without those dairies. Dust only, stale porter fumes, the
brown-flecked baby-tongs of Mrs. Layton-Desmond as she
clutched her ersatz nectar.
   'This is it,' said Jenkins. 'Let's face it. This is it.'
   'Yes dear.'
   'We've got to face it.'
   'What dear?'
   'I do not admit that death,' he began to gobble, 'that death
has dominion over me.'
   'Ah we all thought that dear boy. Such nice boys and girls
some of them were.'
   'Facts, Mrs. Layton-Desmond, facts, for Jesus' sake
give me facts.'
   'Well for instance there was poor Lettie Coogan who
wanted to sing in opera and died eventually in a sweet shop
in Rathgar.'
   'I salute you Lettie.'
   'And there was poor Billy Richards who won ten-and-six
in a poetry competition and died in the Board of Works.'
   'Il miglior fabbro.'
   'And there was poor Johnny Callaghan who was a born
teacher but got himself put in Mountjoy for you know what.'

'The truth is great and will prevail.'

On and on she went, indefatigably threnodic, until she noticed that the glasses were empty and stopped midway through a notice of poor Freddie English who'd wanted to be a priest.

The roll-call was a good sedative for Jenkins. He began to think of the world outside this present. On the pavement outside, Bockety Bill the beggar-man, with an old felt hat, and a little sweet tin, would be leering at the passers-by. Across the road, prim Miss Deeny would be folding papers with her chapped hands, snapping viciously at her customers. A little further away, nuns linked Siamese-like would be twittering home from Keats or Shelley or Wordsworth.

'I'll make it all into a ballad,' said Jenkins firmly. After five minutes by Counihan's contrary old clock he gave up trying to write the ballad. It would have been in the manner of the late Yeats with passionate and simple subject matter. The names in the ballad would have names like Bockety Bill and strong Tom Counihan. He had considered introducing Mrs. Layton-Desmond, and a couple of nuns perhaps, as innovations in ballad personages. He now felt queazyish and went to Counihan's abominable lavatory. He was not comforted by the unsophisticated obscenities on the wall.

When he came back Mrs. Layton-Desmond was sitting at a table in cahoots with two students who each had a pint of stout and a grimy orange Penguin and a folder of protruding notes by way of identification. Jenkins almost retched with reflex hate. What had been *it,* everlasting punishment, infinitely renewable corruption, was now even more so.

'This is Brending,' said Mrs. Layton-Desmond.

'Hello Brendan,' said Jenkins to Brendan. who looked like a startled hare.

'And this is Finting,' she said in a tone which implied she had sons or nephews of her own far away. She had not of course.

'Hello Finting, I mean Fintan,' said Jenkins. Fintan looked more domesticated. But Jenkins was now past caring. *It* was about him and there was no way out to the fields and the hedges and the blackberries, nor to the Green and the daffodils and crocuses.

'What are you reading, Brending?' asked Mrs. Layton-Desmond.

'Evelyn Waugh,' said Brendan. He was looking at Jenkins as if he had two heads.

'And you, Finting?'

'Graham Greene,' said Fintan. He too was looking at Jenkins but more in wonder than in fear.

Mrs. Layton-Desmond focussed her eyes erringly on Jenkins and challenged.

'I understand that dear Evelyn, I knew him when he was a child in Hampstead you know, is very popular among the young of your Alma Mater.'

'You understand correctly,' he said miserably. 'In fact you might say that he has contributed, unwittingly, no doubt, towards the liberalization, in certain connections, of our Catholic young men and women. St. Paul's counsel has gone by the board, and not only is it so much as mentioned amongst them, but indeed it is openly discussed.'

'You can't mean that.'

'I do mean it. Even in my own time there was a disquieting tendency toward flippant remarks about procreation and other mysteries of physical contact between the sexes.'

Quite cheerful now but with tears in his eyes.

'And now,' he boomed, 'I hear it is even worse. Sodom has lost its terrible, its unmentionable repellence and in the conversation of the young has an almost equal footing with Grafton Street, Soho, St. Germain-des Près and the canning factories of our sister island.'

'Quiet, Mr. Jenkins, please,' roared Mr. Counihan, 'it's too early in the day.'

'For what?' asked Mrs. Layton-Desmond.

'For this to happen,' resumed Jenkins. 'Young girls from good homes, some of them with uncles priests and aunts nuns, have been known to make ambiguous remarks, scandalous insinuations, to bandy about the worst excesses of decadent foreign writers totally alien to our native culture and our traditional loyalty to the Holy See.'

'Micheál child, you mustn't fret. It's not for you to bear the burden. You should leave it to boys like Brending and Finting. I'm not a church-goer myself, but I will say I'm shocked by some of the stuff I read nowadays.'

'Is Mr. Jenkins serious?' asked Brendan.

'I think he's pulling our leg,' said Fintan.

Jenkins ignored them.

'Do you believe *Donna* Layton-Desmond, that the dead can love?'

'Yes, dear boy, very much.'

'*Beatrice* Layton-Desmond, my America, my New Found Land.'

'Will you listen to the boy?'

Her eyes glittering with gin appealed to the power that moves the sun and all the stars. She patted her brand new marmalade hair.

'*Fiammetta* Layton-Desmond,' he prayed, 'I love you.'

'Don't say it foolish boy.'

'I will say it,' he thundered. Aloysius Counihan, strictly a twentieth century man, drew in his breath.

'I'll say it on the steps of the Bank of Ireland, I'll shout it to the winds from the steps of the Wellington Monument, I'll have the matter raised in the Dáil, I'll even write letters to the *Irish Times,*' and his voice grew yet louder and thicker, 'I'll hire the beggars of Ireland to blazon it forth at street corners to the vast concourse of the living dead, I'll enter the priesthood and go on the missions, to preach that in all the world, you, *Laura* Layton-Desmond and I, Micheál Jenkins, B.A., B.Comm., we two alone, have been ever, from anyone, absent in the spring.'

Aloysius Counihan moved fast and Jenkins was not his match. He was darkly aware of movement and clatter and Mrs. Layton-Desmond ululating. And then he was outside leaning against the wall with the forward sun too hot on his face.

'Are you all right?' said Brendan.

'Better get something to eat,' said Fintan.

They stayed him with oxtail soup and comforted him with crumpled cigarettes and then one of them gave him his

YARNS
58

writing. There it was on the first page, splotched evilly: 'On
the sham mahogany counter . . .'

'Do you believe in love, Brending, I mean Brendan?' he
asked.

'I suppose I do.'

'And you Fintan, I mean Finting?'

'It depends.'

In the world outside that present, the people were putting
up their umbrellas against the silk rain. Jenkins looked with
tender bleariness at the young asensual faces and was very
grateful that they were not dead.

'How did you get on with Mrs. Layton-Desmond?' he
asked.

'Oh we just met her,' said Brendan.

'She's very generous,' said Fintan.

'When the rain stops we'll go back. It'll be opening time
soon. I want to tell Mrs. Layton-Desmond about the
Resurrection of the Body.'

Passion

They arrived in Seville at six o'clock in the evening and
Dympna was tired after the five-hour bus ride from
Algeciras. She complained also of a pain in her tummy. Bill
sympathized with her fatigue and her pain and bore with her
small moans and injured eyes. He loved his wife. What
completely staggered him was her request for a cup of tea.

For three weeks she had been admirable and Bill had been
proud of her. Not once had she complained about the food
or the water or the lavatories, and Bill's happiness was
increased by the knowledge that his wife — his Dympna —
was sophisticated enough to take the rough with the smooth
in foreign travel. Sometimes in the middle of the night when
Dympna had gone asleep and he lay awake sweating under
their single sheet, he would make up fantasies about their
future married life: Dympna and himself mastering Western
Europe, summer after glittering summer, coming back to
Dublin year after year with stories to dazzle the chaps in the
office and Dympna's girl-friends. But as the light dripped
through the slats, Bill would catch himself on, for there must
and should be children, and he thanked God, in manly
fervour, for this wonderful honeymoon.

The cup of tea worried him. Bill had muddled notions
about conforming to the customs of the country, and he felt
it would be a betrayal of them both to ask for a cup of tea.
But when they were settled in their *pensión de lujo,* which
cost a bit more but was worth it, Dympna's pain went and
she perked up and no more was heard about the cup of tea.

She even hummed to herself while they were washing and changing, and Bill would have liked to look round, but of course did not do so, for after three weeks of marriage they both retained their modesty.

And Dympna looked quite lovely when they went down to dinner, her corn-coloured hair swept back, and her thin-honed shoulders sloping red-brown out of her flared blue cotton. When Bill caught a glimpse of himself in one of the mirrors on the staircase, he thought that he too looked good, with a nice parting in his reddish hair and a smooth tan and a snow-white shirt. You had to hand it to the Spaniards, they got things really white.

When they got to the first turn in the staircase that led to the big roofed *patio,* they almost collided with a young Spaniard. There were bows and retreats and steppings-aside and apologies, and the Spaniard, a smudge of black and olive and white, smiled with what even Bill had to recognise as charm. Dympna's flush came and lingered under her sunburn, and Bill, though proud of being an Irishman, found himself thinking, like a story-book Englishman, that the fellow was too good-looking to be healthy.

In the *patio* other guests were getting up to go in to the dining-room. They were mostly French students, plain, noisy, enthusiastic boys and girls. During the meal they had complicated and fatuous arguments about the temperature of the water, the difference between French and Spanish oils, what they should do and where they should go the day after.

Bill half-listened to them, for though Dympna ate almost greedily and drank more wine than usual, she said nothing beyond 'Pass the salt, please,' and 'This fish is good,' and Bill thought suddenly that they might as well be two strangers seated by chance at the same table. The thought came like a cramp.

'A peach for *la señora?*'

'*Sí, sí.*'

For the first time Bill failed to respond with joy and astonishment to the phrase which more than 'Mrs.' or 'Madame' seemed to establish his new possession and his new way of life. He poured more wine and thought, 'It's too

soon, God, it's too soon.' Around him swelled the din of the
French, as the roar of traffic might reach a patient in a
hospital.

It was half-past ten when they finished dinner. Bill asked
Dympna if she'd like to take a stroll and have some coffee.
She said she was tired and would like to go to bed.

Each new town they had come to, they had wandered a
little on the first night. They had sniffed the mystery of a two
or three-day home, inspecting cafés and marking down
itineraries, cherishing an unexpected silhouette or a
companionable bell. And now in Seville it was different.

Bill was as silent and as nervous as Dympna as they
undressed for bed. To-night she did not ask him to brush her
hair and he did not ask her to scratch his back, a service
which had begun as an urgent request and continued as the
first joke of married life.

Bill stood at the window a moment before drawing the
heavy Venetian blind. He could see below him across the
way through an open window, some negro boys sitting
around a gramophone. He had forgotten about Spain's
colonials. In their happy exile they played old-fasioned
popular tunes of the 'forties. Now it was 'Moonlight becomes
you'. The faded melody, defiant in the city of Moor and Jew
and Christian, made Bill feel tearful and self-pitying and full
of desire. Dympna was in bed now, her hair dull yellow
against the pillow, and lying as she always did while she
waited for him, like an effigy on a tomb. As he turned fully
towards her Bill was shocked by the keenness of his desire and
his sick tenderness. Not even a husband had a right to feel
like this. 'Men, you must learn to master your passions': the
comedian's Cork accent barracked in his ears and at the back
of his nostrils was the attar of incense and body-sweat.

She drew away from him. This had happened twice
before, once for reasons he imperfectly understood but
which he accepted as normal and once because he had gone
off drinking with an American and come back smelling like a
wine-shop. Otherwise she had understood the requirements
of his love, for he was not, as a rule, hot-blooded. Now he
lay on his back beside her and wondered what was wrong.

He watched the shadows on the ceiling, and felt the sweat working down his spine, and his desire and tenderness dwindled into lust and petulance that might have been consoled anywhere.

The negroes continued to play their sweet stale tunes, and the bells of midnight began to perform, silver after silver, gold after gold, and then what must be the imperial decent bronze of the Cathedral.

And then after the confusion of the bells, Bill thought that he was having delusions. He imagined he heard 'The Londonderry Air' played on a trumpet. But he realized it must be another record from across the way. As the trumpet yearned to the top notes, Bill's eyes began to smart and he reached out his hand to Dympna. She did not move.

The shadows were losing ground on the ceiling. He thought about other shadows: the chestnut tree on the lawn where he first kissed her, jumping fire-light when he proposed to her, the watery moon in the Left Bank hotel room . . . He looked at his watch. It was half-past one. Dympna seemed to be asleep.

He got up quietly and groped his way to his hold-all. He rummaged until he found the flask of cognac which he had not touched since Paris. He felt as he had not felt since he first stayed out all night at home, and crept back to safety before light. Guilty, exultant, chilled.

After the first slug he became a little weepier. 'Christ,' he thought, 'what makes it worse, you can't even get drunk in Spain.' And he felt homesick for the chaps in the office and the stag binges and the squalid half-virgin fumblings with ginny girls. He slugged again. A warm, safe, untidy world, and a damned sight better than standing half-naked in a Spanish hotel-room, swilling cognac furtively while your unfriendly wife slept or pretended to sleep in your marriage bed.

He realized that he had finished the bottle and groped his way back to the bed. He tossed and thumped until Dympna thought he would never stop and then, suddenly, he dropped asleep, as the bull drops dead.

She could, by turning her head slightly, see the outlines of his jaw and a shadow of hair, and a glisten of sweat on his chest where his jacket had fallen open, and she smelt the cognac from his breath. She stretched out her hand, then drew it back. Slowly, laboriously, like an infant being rehearsed by the nuns, she made the Sign of the Cross. She twisted her left elbow so as not to disturb Bill.

For the fifth time that night she prayed for strength against temptation, telling on her fingers the Sorrowful Mysteries, meditating as best she could on the Agony, the Scourging, the Crowning and the Carrying. She had reached the Crucifixion when her sore eye-lids gave up the ghost. She fell asleep before the image of a young Spaniard on a Cross, all black and olive and white except for the purple at the hands and feet and side. In her dreams she kissed the feet, and covered them with her corn-coloured hair.

First Draft

'I propose,' said Mrs. Rose McMenamin 'to give up the drink.' She used her most exciting Tipperary contralto.

'O Rose, thou art sick,' her companion said heavily.

'Nonsense,' she ground out, 'I had very little last night.'

They were crossing College Green, despite the fact that the Civic Guard on point-duty was holding up his hand against them. Enemies of Mrs. McMenamin, and her enemies were many and from dissimilar stations of life, claimed that she did these foolish things on purpose: what speedier way of clicking with handsome young policemen? And sure enough while cars trumpeted and squealed and pedestrians helter-skeltered, the Guard, moving with an incomprehensible senility (for he was young and looked quite fit), came up to Mrs. McMenamin and her companion.

'What do you think you're doing, Madam?' he said as coldly as his Southern voice, buttery and vegetable, would allow.

She was certainly a fine figure of a woman. Her figure cut her out to play a Principal Boy of the Old School, her colouring was colleen, raven hair and blue eyes with curling lashes, and she was about thirty-eight in a good light. Beside her, the Guard looked fragile, boyish, consumable. Mrs. McMenamin's companion, a small man with a white blob of face over an almost perfect crescent from collar-stud to belt-buckle, tried to step out of the limelight.

But the Guard added, *'And* ?'

'Oh Gárda,' said Mrs. McMenamin, as if she were

speaking the opening phrase of a Gaelic lyric, possibly one of the Love Songs of Connacht, 'I'm *very* sorry. We were having a most interesting conversation, and were quite *oblivious.*' The last word, lest it sound too hoity-toity, was spoken in the thickest of brogues.

'Well, don't try that class of thing again,' said the Guard, dazzled by that thick-lashed blue eye with its hint of chaste passion. 'And you,' he snarled at the companion. 'Or,' he mumbled half-heartedly, 'you'll be summonsed.'

'Oh dotey, we promise.' Mrs. McMenamin at this moment looked as if she might fall on the Guard's neck and eat him. This disaster, the sort of thing prayed for by her enemies, and constantly being averted by her few but unfashionably loyal adherents, did not of course happen, largely, it was said later by the enemies, because the Guard turned around and ran. In fact the young man realized that unless he got back to his post, traffic in Dublin would be at an indefinite stand-still. He scowled unbecomingly and still moving at the pace of a decrepit ancient, wnet back to the centre of the Green.

'Oh Roddy,' whispered Mrs. McMenamin, 'isn't he wonderful?'

'Handsome is as handsome does,' said Roddy, who was familiar with this kind of thing, and besides was getting on in life.

They linked arms and walked in the direction of Grafton Street. She was about two inches taller than Roddy, and moved with what she may have considered Italianate grace. It cannot be said that Roddy, in his shapeless belly-defined tweeds, could ever be included among popular notions of the *cavaliere servente.* But Mrs. McMenamin had once picked up a boy on the Spanish Steps in Rome, who had insited on addressing her as "Contessa". And nowadays, when she was drunk, her friends were accustomed to her special wee-girl tight voice babbling away about Paolo and how he'd brought her roses and *chianti* and called her *contessa.* 'I was in love,' she would say 'but I knew from the start it was impossible.'

'To get back,' said Roddy, 'what, in the unlikely event of total abstention from drink, do you propose to do?'

He had known her for twenty years but was flabbergasted

by her reply.

'I propose,' she said, 'to devote my life to literary work.'

Her eyes were exceptionally blue, as when she'd reached the half-bottle stage, and now she looked up at a sky that matched them. For it does not always rain in Dublin, not even in the Summer.

They were half-way up Grafton Street before he asked her the nature of the proposed literary work.

'First,' she said, 'I shall write my memoirs. And then some novels, and perhaps a play — a play about my childhood in South Tipperary. After all that cow Mollie Brannigan has written a play about her childhood in West Cork. And if she can do it, I most certainly can.'

'But first your memoirs?'

'Yes, certainly my memoirs will come first.' She appeared to have forgotten her resolution about drinking, for she said suddenly, 'I'd like a drink.'

They turned into a frightful pub. It was long and narrow, and were it not so high, might have been likened to a coffin. As it was, the patrons claimed that it was once a morgue.

It was now noon, and a session was in progress. Sitting on high stools, assorted fringe intellectuals were discussing form and abusing each other. The greatest volume of noise came from a venerable old soul with rich blue-grey moustaches, who was waving a glass of whiskey and spilling most of it over a young man in a bright red shirt and tight pale blue jeans. The young man seemed quite undisturbed by the damp stains accumulating on his stork-thin legs. When Mrs. McMenamin galleoned in, he leaped from his stool and embraced her. The venerable old soul downed his drink with a manic gesture, spat on the ground, and wheeled dangerously on his stool.

'Oh Rose, and Roddy,' said the young man, 'you know Thomas.'

'*Of course,* I know Thomas,' said Mrs. McMenamin warmly. 'Three — no, four — large Jamesons.'

'Jameson Twelve,' roared Thomas, and pacified by the arrival of the drinks, he grumped, 'You're a good girl Rosie, you're a good girl.'

'And how are you, Thomas?' said Mrs. McMenamin.

'Poorly,' said Thomas.

Mrs. McMenamin slipped a pound into the hand of the red-and-pale blue young man. 'Get some more, dotey,' she whispered unnecessarily.

'And what are you doing with yourself these days?' asked Thomas, his eyes squinting horribly.

'I am thinking of writing my memoirs,' said Mrs. McMenamin.

Thomas fell off his stool. When recovered and reinstalled he was remarkably calm except for a reference in reverent tones, to Christ Almighty.

'What class of memoirs would you have in mind?' he asked reasonably.

'Well dotey, you know the kind of thing, my childhood in South Tip, and then school and College in Dublin, and then being a "Miss" in Spain, and my marriage with poor Joe and —' she finished quite shyly, 'the men I've known.'

'It'll be good,' said Thomas magesterially, 'it'll be good.'

'Marvellous,' said the young man, whose jeans continued to be spattered with whiskey.

'Yes', said Roddy.

'Do you really think so?' said Mrs. McMenamin.

'I do,' said Thomas, breaking his glass as he laid it down. 'You have experience, the knowledge, the talent — but have you the Gift?'

'The Gift?'

'Yes.'

'Yes. The Gift. The Light. The Spark. The Flame. The Glory. The Thing. The Sine Qua Non.'

'Do you mean,' said Mrs. McMenamin doubtfully, 'have I the Touch?'

'God, God, God,' Thomas howled, 'the bloody woman understands me. Yes. The Touch. The Fire. The Inexpressible. The Irreducible. The Inexplicable. The *Untouchable*.' And his voice, horrible and splendid in volume, caused the proprietor, who was a nervous man, to give too much change to an awed chimney-sweep, who in turn didn't even notice.

The session then got somewhat out of hand. Towards one
o'clock Thomas conceived, for no reason at all, that they
were on board ship, the *Titanic* perhaps, and that they were
going down. Passers-by were alarmed by cries of 'Batten
down the hatches,' 'Women and children first,' and most
frequent, 'Get back or I'll shoot.' At a quarter-past two they
were singing "Faith of Our Fathers", Thomas having
objected on sectarian grounds to "Nearer, My God, to
Thee". When the proprietor piped 'Time, Gentlemen, Time',
Mrs. McMenamin burst into tears and said that she was a
lady, a *contessa* in fact, and she told the red-and-pale blue
young man who was known normally as "Petie" but whom
she insisted now on calling "Pietro", all about Rome and
Paolo and the roses and the *chianti,* and though he had
heard it all before, he was enraptured, despite half a large
whiskey in his hair, poured by Thomas in an effort to check
flames spreading from the engine-room. Petie was a
romantic young man.

By the time they left, the proprietor was falling back on
'Last boat, gentlemen, last boat,' and Petie had been busy on
the telephone. As a result there was a taxi waiting. Roddy
went in front with the driver and Mrs. McMenamin sat
behind between Petie and Thomas. Roddy gave
directions

There was peace.

'Who's this bastard?' said Thomas suddenly.

'Do you mean Petie?' said Mrs. McMenamin.

'I mean this bastard,' said Thomas.

'Oh but Petie's a dote.'

'Is that a fact, do you tell me that,' said Thomas.

'Yes,' said Mrs. McMenamin. 'Petie's in theatre, in
London .

'Oh that must be very interesting,' said Thomas. 'They're
terrible cute in London.'

'I'll say they are,' said Petie.

Thomas fell back in amiable disgust. He did not speak
again until they were established in a little pub far out of
Dublin, and then it was to a group of tinkers with whom he
discussed the mending of pots and the stealing of hens. He

accepted the large whiskies sent across but otherwise ignored
Mrs. McMenamin, Roddy and Petie. Mrs. McMenamin
turned to De Kuypers' gin, because she had persuaded
herself that the barman, a simple red-haired young man,
resembled a Dutch boy she'd picked up in a bar in
Amsterdam.

'I was in love,' she said, 'but I knew from the start it was
impossible.'

'Rosie darling,' said Roddy gently, 'surely that was
another time.'

'Nonsense,' she shouted, 'I've been in love many times,
and almost *always* from the start I've known it was
impossible.'

An elephantine roar from Thomas brought the redhaired
barman from behind the counter.

'This is poison,' said Thomas and he poured his whiskey
into one of the tinkers' pints of stout. 'I won't drink another
drop unless it's from a sealed bottle.' He then fell asleep on
the table.

'Dear Thomas,' said Mrs. McMenamin.

'I think he's such a sweet old boy,' said Petie.

'Yes,' said Roddy.

'Yes,' said Mrs. McMenamin. 'I've been in love many
times.'

The familiar remembering sheen was coming over her big
blue eyes. In a single poem, a minor Irish poet, who later
died in an attack of *delirium tremens,* had compared their
blue with the Neopolitan blue of Killiney Bay and
the minatory blue of the Atlantic seen before a storm from a
little Western bay. There had also been references to corn-
flowers, bluebells and the robe of Our Lady. To her great
credit Mrs. McMenamin had not taken this poem very
seriously.

'Many times,' she said. Now that Thomas's honkings had
stopped, the little pub was very quiet. The tinkers had gone,
and the redhaired barman was nodding over the racing-page
of *The Irish Press.* The sunshine outside was no reminder of
a world elsewhere, even though it poured through the open
door, making chiaroscuro where Thomas lay, and dreamed

perhaps of horses or of epic poems or of beautiful ladies. The
three drinkers were immune from the distractions of a fine
August afternoon in the Dublin countryside, from the
sunshine and the blending greens and the white road and the
sky as blue as Mrs. McMenamin's eyes.

'Even poor Joe,' she said. 'I think I even really loved
poor Joe. God knows he loved me. And anyway he left me
well-off. Perhaps it's as well there was no child. I can't
imagine why. But there, it was God's will, as Father Kevin
used to say. We certainly went to all the best doctors, Jo-Boy
Carmody and Bennie Harris and Tod Mercer and the rest.'

She turned suddenly to Roddy and pressed his hand.

'Oh dotey,' she said, 'you were so good to me when Joe
died.'

'I've loved you for over twenty years,' said Roddy with
dignity.

'I *know,* Roddy, I *know.*'

Thomas turned three times in his sleep and leaped up.

'Whiskey,' he roared.

'Whiskey,' said Mrs. McMenamin.

'Four of the best,' said the redhaired barman.

'Who is this bastard?' said Thomas.

'Do you mean Petie?' said Mrs. McMenamin.

'No, this bastard,' said Thomas, pointing to Roddy.

'Oh Roddy's sweet,' said Mrs. McMenamin. 'He's in tex-
tiles. But he also writes.'

'Do you tell me that? Now that's very interesting. Do you
deal in crepylene?'

'My firm handles it.'

'Oh it's fantastic stuff. I have a pair of trousers made out
of it, and you can do anything with them. You can stamp on
them, tear them, drag them through the hedge backwards,
piss on them. Christ, you could *eat* them. Oh it's fantastic
stuff.'

'Let's go back to town,'   said Mrs. McMenamin, 'We'll
take a taxi.'

But they stopped at many pubs on the way. At one Petie
was sick over a juke-box where he was trying to play a
Johnny Ray record. At another Thomas was refused

service. At another Mrs. McMenamin abused the proprietor for the lack of adequate toilet facilities. At three more Thomas was refused service. At a seventh Mrs. McMenamin told three African students that she was a *contessa*. It was but a short step to eating deplorable *spaghetti* and drinking very expensive *chianti*.

Thomas also had a steak with chips and disgusting tinned peas. He then announced, quite soberly, that he wished to go home financed but unescorted. They saw him into a taxi, with a pound-note in his hand. As the taxi moved away he stuck his head from the window and told them they were nothing but a pack of bastards. They waved affectionately.

'He's such a nice man,' said Mrs. McMenamin.

'Absolutely,' said Petie.

'Yes,' said Roddy.

They were weary from drink. Roddy was grey. Petie was a nasty olive, and Mrs. McMenamin was over-rosy. But in the old gold of the sunlight, they went back to their pub of the morning.

'How lovely Dublin is at six o'clock of a fine Summer's evening,' said Petie, his vapid little face all sweet in the last of the radiance.

'What a great pleasure drinking is,' said Mrs. McMenamin.

'Yes,' said Roddy.

The pub was chock-a-block with business men of the district, with here and there a couple of young men in Tony Curtis hair-styles and bright cheap suits, gulping down stout before going dancing. Roddy poked out seats and ordered whiskey, and they sat silently and uneasily.

'It's been a lovely day,' said Mrs. McMenamin. From habit she kept her eye on the door. Suddenly she manacled Roddy's wrist. She half-rose, then sank back, one hand still around Roddy's wrist, the other towards her breast, the first inevitabe gesture of the tragic mime.

'What's wrong, Rosie?' asked Roddy.

'Oh Roddy, it's him, you know, the. ...'

'The what?'

'Oh Roddy dotey, the *Gárda*.'

Roddy looked across and saw a grave young man in a neat blue suit standing at the bar, drinking a bottle of stout.

'But Rosie darling, he won't harm you. Anyway he wouldn't come in here to summons us. Besides. ...'

'Oh dotey I know that.'

'Well, what's the matter?' But he knew. 'No Rosie, you can't pick up strange young policemen in a bar. It can't be done.'

'But he's not strange. I mean he knows us.'

'No Rosie.'

'But couldn't you just ask him to have a drink, as a sort of *apology* for this morning?'

'No, Rosie, certainly not.'

'Oh please, dotey, for me.'

'All right. But I warn you.'

He went across to the bar, and a moment later came across with the Guard.

'May I present Mrs. McMenamin, Mr. Peter Thorpe and eh. ...'

'O'Halloran.'

'Guard O'Halloran. My name's Rodney Kent.'

'Pleased to meet you.'

'What a pleasure, Gárda, to be able to apologise properly for our *terrible* behaviour this morning. Now what will you have to drink?'

'I'm grand thanks.'

'Oh but you must have a drink with us. A whiskey?'

'No thanks. I never touch the hard stuff.'

There was a terrible roaring sound at the door, and Thomas came hurtling in, throwing out questions in his progress: 'What's the news?' 'Where's everyone?' 'Who's that bastard?'

He repeated the last question as he came abreast of Guard O'Halloran.

'Oh Thomas,' said Mrs. McMenamin, 'this is Guard O'Halloran.'

'Do you tell me that? That's very interesting. A friend of mine had a still in the County Mayo. He told me the police were a terrible lot of bastards.'

'For Christ's sake get Thomas a drink, Roddy,' hissed Mrs. McMenamin, and turning to Guard O'Halloran she said, 'I'm sure it must be very interesting and *dangerous* work.'

'Dangerous me bottom,' said Thomas, 'going around tormenting decent innocent Catholic men and women, destroying the ancient traditions, all of them in the pay of de Valera and the Freemasons and the Ashkenazys —'

'The *who?*' asked Petie.

Thomas was so taken aback that after once again bellowing 'Ashkenazys', he was quiet and drank his whiskey.

'Now Gárda,' said Mrs. McMenamin, 'you will have another stout at least.'

'Ah no thanks miss, I have to be pushing off. Thanks all the same.'

'So early?'

'Well you see,' he blushed, 'I have to meet the girl-friend.'

'Girl-friend.'

'Yes, and as you know yourself Miss, ladies don't like to be kept waiting.' He was now flame-cheeked.

'No, they don't.'

'You look to me like a nice young fellow,' said Thomas.

'Well goodnight all, and I'm pleased to have met you.'

He had turned away when suddenly he smiled back at Mrs. McMenamin, with an expression of ridiculous archness, 'Be more careful in future in College Green. I'll be watching for you.'

He'd gone.

'A nice young fellow,' said Thomas.

'Oh Rose, oh Rose,' said Roddy. 'Why did you do it?' She was crying.

'Give me a penny,' she said, 'I'll be back in a moment.'

'That woman has the Gift,' said Thomas fiercely. 'Them memoirs of hers will be fantastic stuff, *fantastic*. A friend of mine once wrote a book of memoirs, all about life on the farm. But that woman's will be better, because she has the Gift.'

In the taxi home, after they had dropped first Petie and then Thomas, Mrs. McMenamin looked at Roddy, and she seemed sober.

'I'm in love,' she said, 'and I know from the start it's impossible.'

'Oh Rose, oh Rose.'

About the same time Thomas began to clatter dementedly on his typewriter, and by four o'clock had produced the first draft of one of his noblest poems.

In it he spoke of things he did not need to see and knew from the start to be possible. Of the sunshine and the blending greens, of the white road and the sky as blue as Mrs. McMenamin's eyes.

Poetry Ireland

After dinner, the guests pottered out on to the veranda. The veranda overlooked a long narrow garden which in June was heavy with the warm winey odour of roses but which was now, in September, a confused mass of briars and dry leaves. Electric light had been installed on the veranda the previous Autumn so that guests could sit about in the twilight and yet have light enough to read.

This evening was very warm and there was a smell like freshly-made milk chocolate in the air. The mountains showed purple between the branches of the quiet trees at the end of the garden. A great disc of flame hung in the sky.

Mr. O'Shea came out, his little full mouth moving soundlessly as he read from a book of poetry. He flopped into a basket chair and with the jolt his pince-nez slipped a fraction of an inch down his nose. He wore a pair of meticulously creased flannels and a sports-coat of impeccable taste. He was a shade too thick around the hips for a man of his age. Mr. O'Shea was thirty-one.

Mrs. Mahaffey, the proprietress, was standing at the glass door and as the guests came out she shouted into their ear.

'Are any more chairs needed? For the love o' God, make sure o' how many yez want and don't have poor Larry traipsin' in and out, when he wants to get off home to his unfortunate wife and the ninth just arrived.'

She was a great strapping woman with hair like ripe corn and while she spoke she ran her big hands through it. When she had finished speaking she stood waiting for an answer, her hands on her swelling hips.

'One more chair, Mrs. Mahaffey, please,' said Mrs. MacMorris, 'I'd like to rest the old leg. It's conking out again. Coralie, did you see my bag?'

'No, indeed, Miss MacMorris, I didn't see your bag,' said Coralie, 'but sure maybe you left it inside?' Coralie wrinkled up her narrow pasty forehead, and her colourless china eyes looked old and tired. Miss MacMorris poked about under her chair.

'Did you lose anything?' said Mrs. Drennan.

'I'm looking for my bag,' said Mrs. MacMorris.

'Did you leave it inside?' said Mrs. O'Hara.

'I'll go in and look,' said Coralie and she walked in, in her odd, jerky, marionette fashion.

Mrs. Mahaffey was down in the garden now.

'Here puss, here puss, here puss,' she whispered as she searched the briars. The trees were swaying gently. The sun was dying on the horizon in a welter of red, and little wisps of green, like scraps from a greensilk knitted blouse, were drifting about on the silver clouds.

Mr. Coleman threw his paper on the floor and said in a voice like a creaking door, 'Five and a quarter million a year goes on gambling and twenty million on drink in this country each year.'

Coralie brought out Miss MacMorris's bag. 'It was under your chair in the diningroom,' she said, and the sound of her voice was unnatural and strained, on that veranda where everyone but Mr. O'Shea was over fifty.

'Thank you, Coralie,' said Miss MacMorris and she took out a cigarette case made of green lacquer, filled with little pungent cigarettes that made the air drowsy with their heavy scent.

'Twenty-five and a quarter million,' said Mr. Coleman. 'Aren't we a marvellous people? With a population of less than three million? It'd make you sick.' He shook his head like a dog coming out of the canal, and a little squeaky titter that rose into a loud, peculiar laugh came from the corner where Coralie sat, her body half-obscured by the smoke of Miss MacMorris's cigarettes.

Mrs. Mahaffey down in the garden was calling softly, 'Here puss, here puss,' and Mr. O'Shea caught glimpses of her massive yellow head. The silver clouds darkened and the stray wisps of green were lost. A breeze was blowing lazily through the trees at the end of the garden. From the shadows that lay about the town down the road at the foot of the chalky hill, little farthings of light were flickering.

'My heart is like a singing bird,' said Mr. O'Shea softly.

'What's that?' said Mr. Coleman sharply.

'Oh, just poetry,' said Mr. O'Shea.

'Oh, poetry,' said Mrs. Drennan.

'Very nice if you have a taste for it, but it doesn't do to become too fond of it,' said Mrs. O'Hara. She had a heavy placid face and there was a steely point in her pale blue bovine eyes.

No-one answered her. Mrs. Mahaffey was whispering to the kitten which at last she had found and was feeding with a saucer of cream. 'Drink it all up, puss, there's a good puss.'

Mrs. O'Hara continued, 'My girls used to be very fond of poetry when they were going to school. The nuns used to give them a good course of it.'

'Oh yes,' said Coralie, 'the nun we had at school was very keen on poetry. "The Daffodils" and "The Lady of Shalott". She was a scream. We were always laughing at her. She used to have to read the rolls in Irish and she used to mix up the Irish and English together. Oh, we had great fun entirely.' Her slight frame shook with laughter and her cheeks were like pink chalk. She bent down to fasten her shoelace and her brown hair fell out of the pink bow and got into her eyes. She raised her head and she muttered in a half-ashamed voice, 'Oh my back.' She paused to breathe and went on, 'I remember talking about Sister Madeleine to Father Lynch at the Fête last year. We had a great talk. I sold him a book of tickets for a raffle for a baby doll. "What would I do with a baby doll?" said he. "Oh," said I, "you could raffle it for the Church in Ballymocderg." He nearly died laughing.' Coralie's colourless china eyes were met with laughter.

Long black clouds were breaking up in the sky; in the

town the farthings of light were beginning to blaze.

'It was a great affair, the Fête. Miss MacMorris had some lovely stuff. Though indeed the Legion of Mary had a stall next door and they hadn't much. But they're a dangerous crowd, the Legion. You daren't say a word but they're off to Father Creed, and start telling him all sorts.' Coralie bent forward and her face was vivid with remembrance.

'What was that bit of poetry, Mr. O.?' said Mrs. Drennan, 'the bit about the bird.'

'My heart is like a singing bird,' said Mr. O'Shea.

'That sounds a bit queer,' said Coralie. 'But it's very nice, isn't it? Still, it's a bit queer.'

'Is there no more of it, Mr. O.? said Mrs. Drennan.

'Yes,' said Mr. O'Shea, 'there's more of it,

"My heart is like a singing bird
Whose nest is in a watered shoot,
My heart is like an apple-tree
Whose boughs are bent with thick-set fruit." '

'What's that about?' said Mr. Coleman.

'Oh, it's beautiful,' said Mrs. Drennan.

'Very far-fetched, it seems to me,' said Mrs. O'Hara.

'Oh, I think it's lovely entirely,' said Coralie, and her colourless china eyes were wet again.

'It was written by a woman in love,' said Mr. O'Shea.

Down at the end of the garden the trees made little whispering noises, and the clouds slipped away until the sky had the sheen of black velvet. A scrap of moon, like a slice of tinned pear, slid through a crevice in the darkness, and the stars, like pieces of tinsel from a Christmas tree, gleamed on the garden.

'Isn't it a gorgeous night, Mrs. O'Hara?' said Mrs. Drennan. 'A real peaceful night, thanks be to God for it.'

'Twenty-five and a quarter million . . .' said Mr. Coleman, 'why doesn't the cursed Government put a cripplin' tax on gamblin' and the consumption of alcoholic liquors? That'd soon stop it.'

'Oh, Mr. Coleman, you're a hard man,' said Coralie, 'a bit like Mr. Roddy, the man livin' next to Miss MacMorris. He helped us at the Fête . . . but sure he was really very nice.

When I was helping Jimmy Carter put up the little coloured flags on the stall, said Mr. Roddy, "You're a quare long time about a couple o' flags." Oh, I nearly collapsed. Mr. Roddy, too, used always be complaining about the drink and the dogs. Still I do have to laugh at the men coming out of the bars . . .' She broke off with a shriek of laughter.

Miss MacMorris shivered and said, 'Are you coming in, Coralie? It's getting chilly.' She got up and her face was white except for the little reddish veins in her cheeks.

'I think I'll go in too,' said Mrs. O'Hara, 'the breeze is getting sharp.'

'Indeed it is,' said Mrs. Drennan, 'and I have a bit of a cold on me too.'

The garden was full of whisperings and rustlings. Mrs. Mahaffey had forgotten to bring in the saucer. It lay in the track of a thin ray of moonlight, white and gleaming.

Mr. O'Shea and Mr. Coleman were left on the veranda.

'What was that about the bird?' said Mr. Coleman.

'Oh, just poetry,' said Mr. O'Shea.

'My wife has one of them yellow canaries. The bloody thing's a hell of a nuisance.'

'Quite so,' said Mr. O'Shea.

Not Quite The Same

'Aye,' said Thomas.

'And then,' said Mrs. McMenamin, eyes French-polished with intense recollection, 'then, they gave the mouse to the dog, a poodle it was, very badly kept, but not, I would have thought, *given* to mice.'

'A decent beast,' said Thomas.

'O Thomas,' she cried, 'you put things so well.'

'So well you might say,' said Thomas. He was getting restive. Before Mrs. McMenamin had time to draw in her bosom for another episode about the poodle and the mouse, he let out a ferocious blast compounded of yawn, snarl, growl, screech, threnody, ode, hallelujah, belch. Thomas was invoking Our Blessed Lord.

'No singing,' said Dr. Dargan, a venerable person who had abandoned for the licensing trade a distinguished career as a general practitioner. He was hard of hearing.

'I'm not singing,' said Thomas humbly.

'Sounded very like it to me,' said Dr. Dargan. Eyes like perished finger-tips dared Thomas to answer back. He didn't, but when Dr. Dargan had wheeled about and in the pretence of washing glasses, was making frantic sweeps with an odious cloth, Thomas bent over to Mrs. McMenamin and said, 'Rose, I'd be nervous of that fellow. I'm sure he's a sex maniac.'

'O no,' she said, and she put her hand on her heart.

'What I want to say is this,' said Thomas, and as he tongued his splendid moustaches he took on the look of a dead ringer for Dr. Schweitzer.

'Well now, as I was saying ...' Mrs. McMenamin opened her mouth and Thomas began to sing a hymn called, 'I'll sing a hymn to Mary.' Mrs. McMenamin assumed a devotional expression and were it not that she had one hand about a glass of brandy, she would unquestionably have joined it with the other. Those Homeric blue eyes brimmed, those impossible lashes quivered, that masterpiece of a mouth champed a little. Five minutes or so and the sacrifice of Melchisedech would be consummated and little Rose, dear little sweet little so winning Rose, would be walking the streets of Paradise. 'I'll love and bless Thy name,' Thomas wound up with gusto. From around the corner, like an orchestrated ass's bray, came the blind fiddler's rendition of 'The Blue Danube'. Through the window Mrs. McMenamin could see a stopped clock and a hideous brick building the colour of rose in an unnatural late sunlight. Dr. Dargan was muttering to himself, and his apprentice was scurrying about doing nothing. He had an odd hairstyle and wore badly-scuffed winkle-pickers. His name was Aubrey and he was a great admirer of Mrs. McMenamin.

'It's not quite the same,' said Mrs. McMenamin.

'What's that you say?' growled Thomas.

'That hymn,' she gulped. 'When I think of My Childhood, and Thomas, it meant so much to me, and you know I really am religious, and Roddy   you remember darling Roddy? — says he thinks I need the Church and he *really* loves me.'

'That fellow Roddy,' said Thomas benignly, 'talks too much about love.'

'How can you say such a thing,' said Mrs. McMenamin. She was genuinely aghast.

'I mean to say, you can talk about horses or drink or women, but you never talk about love.' He cleared his throat genteely, and carefully de-irrigated his moustaches with a large scarlet handkerchief on which was picked out in yellow the word 'Miami'.

'Thomas,' she said, 'you disappoint me.'

'You disappoint me. Aubrey,' he exploded. He pronounced the first syllable to rhyme with 'cow'.

'Yes sir,' said Aubrey.

'Give us a large Jameson Ten and whatever that woman wants.'

'Brandy,' said Mrs. McMenmin peevishly. She objected, on the soundest possible principles, to being called a woman, and especially by Thomas who most of the time was a perfect gentleman. Aubrey brought the drinks and waited while Thomas dug deep into the caverns of his ducks. A couple of pious ejaculations assisted in the production of a ten-shilling note. Aubrey swooped and in full descent was clutched by a hand of gun-metal.

'Manners,' said Thomas paternally. 'A young fellow like you cannot get on without manners. Christ, where did you get those shoes?'

'They're winkle-pickers. Did you never hear of them?'

'I did indeed.' He swivelled and bayed, 'Is that yourself, Packy.' Packy came crab-wise in his decent professional suit and said, 'I'm very glad to see you Thomas, and you Mrs. McMenamin.'

'Twelve-and-four,' said Aubrey.

'You'll be paid,' said Thomas. 'Now Packy, you're a highly sophisticated and knowledgeable fellow. You've been to three schools and the U.C.D. You'd know about winkle-pickers.'

'Yes indeed Thomas,' said Packy.

'Well now, there's a young fellow comes in here. A young fella,' he said disgustedly. 'He wears a kind of shoe, a bit like Aubrey's there.'

'Oh yes,' said Packy. 'He wears elephant-skin sawn-off winkle-pickers.'

'I remember particularly the lovely gnawing sensation coming back from Communion,' said Mrs. McMenamin. She was not interested in winkle-pickers. She could not see their relevance to the human heart. 'I grew up, and you know, it wasn't quite the same.'

'You're perfectly right,' said Thomas. 'But I'd love to know how they got the elephant-skin.'

'You know I'm not an intellectual,' said Mrs. McMenamin, 'but I love that bit in Colette about coming back from Communion.'

'Elephants are highly intelligent beasts,' said Thomas

'I'll *never* forget the poodle and the mouse,' said Mrs. McMenamin.

'There is no world outside Verona walls,' said Packy absently. On the side he had procured for himself a modest glass of cider. He could be forgiven because he had loved much. In his eyes was the cunning of lost love, the watchfulness of the betrayed.

High above the madness of cars, driving to hell down Grafton Street, the blind fiddler importuned late-shoppers and tourists with 'Peggy O'Neill'. Suddenly there was a purity in the air, a girl's voice true as a lark, testifying to the childhood of Mrs. McMenamin, and to Packy's lost love and to Thomas's inordinate pain at the fate of elephants. 'Did the poodle eat the mouse?' said Thomas.

'All that sand and all that sun and the feeling like hot cocoa in the tummy,' said Mrs. McMenamin. 'I didn't look to see if it ate the mouse.'

'It's a hard world,' said Packy. 'I once had an air-gun and **I shot a thrush. I've never killed anything since.**'

'Except my heart,' said Mrs. McMenamin, with exemplary insincerity.

'I hate that word heart,' said Thomas. His voice was heavy with the doom of the humble. And the lark's voice sang out again and a girl with eyes that were an even truer blue than Mrs. McMenamin's and hair that looked argent in the perverse sunlight stumbled in.

'The poor bitch,' said Packy judicially.

'You pipsqueak you,' said Mrs. McMenamin. 'Poor Primrose — you've got to have heart.'

'I hate that word,' said Thomas. 'What are you having Prim?'

'No singing here,' said Dr. Dargan, dragged out of private madness by a lark's voice.

'Thank you Thomas,' said Primrose, 'I'm very drunk.'

'Indeed you're not,' said Thomas. 'Now Rosie here and Packy and myself were discussing elephants. Do they have those beasts in Spain?'

'I once,' said Primrose, 'saw a drunken elephant.'

'God that must have been very interesting.'

'Aubrey,' said Primrose, 'please give me a drink. I won't sing.'

'You can sing if I'm here,' said Thomas.

'Indeed you may,' said Packy.

Dr. Dargan said that there was to be no bad language. The lark's voice sang out again and intolerable peace descended, light as silk, like the small rains of early spring.

'Love,' said Thomas gloomily.

'Thomas,' said Mrs. McMenamin, 'I hate that word.'

'Aye,' said Thomas. 'I once knew a fella who was in love. A fella a bit like meself. A terrible poor bastard. So I said to him, "Do you know what you can do?" And he said "What?" and I said "Go up to the Zoo".'

And they all thought about animals and themselves. Dr. Dargan rinsed glasses and Aubrey whistled a pop-song and Roddy came in.

II

He had not changed in the two years since Mrs. McMenamin fell in love with the Civic Guard on point-duty, and knew from the start it was impossible. The curve from stud to trouser-belt buckle had not increased, nor had it diminished. But lately he tended to carry his drink unsteadily and although he still worshipped Mrs. McMenamin, yet that acolyte's patience of his was showing signs of wear and tear. When Rose was behaving outrageously he would rap his finger on the table and say, 'You can't go on like this' and she would spit back, 'What right have you to talk to me like this,' and he would say 'Because I love you.' Then on like corny stage-effect would come the tears, and the early more deplorable repertoire of striking gestures and husky vocalization would be played out until he took her home and sat with her until she'd drunk and cried herself to sleep. Sometimes he slept in the spare room and in the very late morning was permitted to assist at the reconstruction of that marvellous face. As he watched the

profile being painted and shadowed back into mature
girlhood, Roddy's tenderness would catch him by the throat
and in that room smelling of *eau-de-cologne* and brandy and
French cigarettes he would live over in stinging minutes the
decades of his service.

'Roddy,' said Thomas, 'come over here.'

'Yes, Thomas?'

'Hold out your hand till I give you a smack'.

'Don't mind him,' said Mrs. McMenamin. Warm,
indulgent, with all her boys about her.

'Roddy,' said Primrose, 'my first and only love.' She had
met him for the first time time ten years ago, and had got it
into her head that he had, as she put it, 'taken quite a fancy'
to her.

'Great God,' said Thomas. He was about to let loose on
Primrose when a new round came up in double-quick time.
Dr. Dargan considered that Roddy was a gentleman, and in
his case service was uninterrogated and speedy.

'Rose,' said Roddy. 'I've bad news for you.'

'O no.' She got the hand to her heart too quickly.

'I called for you this morning,' he let this sink in, 'and Mr.
App bearded me in the hall.'

'That App,' said Thomas, 'is a scoundrel. What's worse
he's a fraud.'

'He's coming in here to look for you, Rose.'

'I've paid my rent.' A great and gallant lady.

'He says you must stop offering insults to his wife when
you are intoxicated.'

'App was in Africa,' said Thomas, 'or maybe in India. He
must know a fair share about elephants.'

'I can't see why App should care,' said Mrs. McMenamin.
'He treats that poor Leah like dirt.'

'He says your comments on her study of the Works of
Shakespeare upset her very much. She's very sensitive.'

'She calls me in,' said Mrs. McMenamin fiercely. 'I can't
pass her bloody door but she pops out and insists I have a
snifter from her gin-bottle. Yesterday,' she glowed, 'I was up
early. Half-past nine. I *crept* past the door but out she came
and it was half-past ten before I got away. She was reading

The Merchant of Venice and so naturally I made a little joke about Leah and the wilderness of monkeys. I suppose she told Nugent App I compared him to Shylock.' She swigged and said happily, 'I wish I had.'

'Where did App get that Leah?' said Thomas.

'He says he met her on tour in the Provinces,' said Mrs. McMenamin. 'I don't believe she's his wife at all.'

'You might be right there,' said Thomas. 'Many illicitous unions are contracted by mummers. I remember there was a fellow used to come down the country with a performing bear. One day he was there, and the next he was gone, and the cobbler's daughter with him. There were some people said she was eaten by the bear, but they were seen afterwards, the three of them, in Wigan, Lancs., by a fellow from the neighbourhood. Her face was destroyed with paint and you could see a fair amount of her bosom. Shockin' altogether.'

'Mind you,' said Packy, who had been whispering in the little pink ear of Primrose, 'I've heard that Nugent was once a very good actor and that he gave up a career in the West End to look after Leah, who isn't his wife, but his mother'.

'Don't be ridiculous,' said Mrs. McMenamin. 'App's too old to be her son.'

'You'd never know,' said Packy, 'with that yellowy face of hers. He's about fifty-five. If she was seventy she could have had him when she was fifteen.' A little in drink, Packy's prose became less formal and his careful legal voice took on the shrewd lilt of his native parts.

Something had electrified Dr. Dargan. He belted around the counter to the door, where half-way through, a hand almost entirely hidden by a great folly of white lilac, was trying to push in. Dr. Dargan yanked back the door viciously and a very odd person plunged through. White lilac foamed about the torso and most of the face, and from the other hand dangled a string bag which appeared to contain jam-pots.

'Thank you, thank you,' said the person in a high silvery voice. 'God bless you, God bless.'

'App,' said Packy.

'Nugent App,' said Mrs. McMenamin.

'The low bastard,' said Thomas.

'Ah my darlings,' said App, and the lilac and the jam-pots were dumped with a swish and a clatter on the counter.

'Rose my love, Thomas my dear fellow, Packy you naughty boy you, Roddy my old faithful and — do I know this little lady?' He leered at Primrose.

'I don't want to know a man who married his mother.'

'Oh boys oh boys,' chanted App. 'What a pretty wit you have. If only my Leah could hear you!'

'Take that bloody lilac out of my way,' said Thomas.

'It's for you Rose!' sang App. 'I picked it this morning on the way back from an early elocution class in the Convent of the Most Immaculate. All the way back to Fitzwilliam Square I carried it, and all the way here.'

'What are the jam-jars for?' asked Packy.

'Returns, dear, returns. Bloody empties. Tuppence each pot. My Leah's such an economical housekeeper, which reminds me, Rose angel honey-bunch, what with her housework and her intensive study of the Works of Shakespeare, my Leah mustn't be upset by your naughty remarks. Why dear she said that you said I was like Shylock. Me dear! A wild spendthrift like me!'

This performance was given in a voice of campanile splendour, except when it cracked. De-lilaced, Mr. App displayed a fine physique and a thinning mane of chemically black hair. He wore an orange shirt with a black tie, a royal blue suit and tan suede shoes. He had a gold wristlet watch and a gold wedding ring, and he used a gold lighter for a Turkish cigarette from a gold case which he did not offer.

'O Nugent,' said Mrs. McMenamin, 'don't bother me about Leah. You know I don't care and I know you don't mean it.'

'Never mind dear. It's my birthday.'

An angel passed over and then Thomas asked, 'How old are you App?'

'Thirty-nine my dear fellow, but I feel nineteen!'

'Lord give me patience,' said Thomas.

'Keep the bright side up,' said Packy.

'It makes it all the worse marrying your mother,' said
Primrose.

'O Nugent,' said Mrs. McMenamin, 'you'll be the death
of me.'

'And what's more, I'm having a few darlings in for drinks
at eight and I want you *all* to come — yes dear, even the little
lady who thinks I'm what's-his-name, that Greek boy you
know.'

He was gone, clattering his jam-jars, his stolen lilac
already wilting on the counter, bells echoing in all their
heads. Dr. Dargan came up muttering, 'I'll have to get rid of
this rubbish,' and bundled up the blossoms for the dust-bin.

'I don't believe it,' said Mrs. McMenamin.

'Wonders will never cease,' said Packy.

'I forgot to ask him about the elephants,' said Thomas.

'We're not going,' said Roddy.

'Why,' said Primrose, 'I've never had drinks with a man
that married his mother.'

'It'll be cup,' said Mrs. McMenamin, 'cup made of cider
and meths.'

'It'd drive us all mad,' said Thomas. 'I once knew a fellow
who drank meths and he ended up thinking he was a tram,
passengers and all. He emigrated to Hong Kong and turned
into a rickshaw.'

'What's the address?' said Primrose, and began to sing.
But the lark seemed to have a cold and Thomas said, 'For
Christ's sake shut up or go up to the Zoo. Roddy there'll run
you up.'

III

Of course they went to Nugent App's, but not before
Packy had attempted to swing from a chandelier in a high-
class restaurant and got them put out. Roddy said that
something seemed to have got into Packy that night and
Thomas said 'Drink.' Mrs. McMenamin said that he certainly
did not seem to be himself, and Primrose six times expressed
the view that the fellow was not quite right in the head. When
she opened her mouth to say this a seventh time, Packy took

her hand lovingly and bit it.

She was still moaning, 'He bit my hand,' when they arrived at ten o'clock in Fitzwilliam Square. App flung open the door to them and carilloned, 'Come in, come in, I've a sup taken, and I have a lovely surprise for you all, you sweet crowd of perfect ducks.' There was a greenish glitter in his eyes and Primrose whispered audibly, 'I think he's the Devil.'

The house in Fitzwilliam Square was owned by Nugent App, or jointly by App and Leah, or perhaps only by Leah, no-one knew. Mrs. McMenamin rented the top floor, the middle floors were let to girls who went out to business, App and Leah had the ground floor, and in the basement lived two aging young men of reserved disposition referred to by App as Dot and Carry. Occasionally he would go downstairs and harangue them about the decline in the marriage rate, the joys of conjugal love, and their duty to the Nation. App had never squashed the yarn that years ago in Seville he had gotten a gipsy with child and in moments of exceptional sentiment he would sob about his little Juanito.

'Come along my darlings,' screeched App, 'you'll be thrilled.'

The room was littered with very young men and women. There was a sound like the humming of bees as they wooed each other daringly and asexually. Some of them held glasses containing an amberish liquid. In a corner an interesting figure was whisking ferociously and at random in several huge glass jugs. It was Leah. She wore a very low-cut gown that hung perfectly vertical from her large yellow shoulders. Her powderless face was wounded with lipstick, and on her head she carried an enormous blonde wig.

'O God, it's the Cup,' said Mrs. McMenamin.

'Let me out of here,' howled Thomas, but App clutched him by the shoulder so powerfully that he froze in motion, one leg lifted, manic horror on his face.

'Silence,' yodelled App. The bees stopped. 'I want you,' App began, 'I want you all to know and love each other — here are Thomas whose divine work you all know, and Rose who is something more in my life than a mere tenant, and Packy who handles all our little legal difficulties, and Roddy who's an Old Faithful, and this bewitching creature who thinks I married my mother, called Violet or Jasmine or something — and these,' he swung his fine white hand around the room, 'these are some of my Past Pupils, grand boys and girls from the Top Schools of Ireland who never forget their Dear Old Teacher who taught them the Art of Noble Speech, and some of them in the theatre themselves now, the dears.'

'In the Name of Suffering —' moaned Thomas.

'You don't have to drink the Cup,' hissed App.

'Over by the window-seat with you all and I'll bring you Jameson Ten and Cork Gin and Pernod. I fecked masses of bottles at darling Birdie Bernstein's the other night. One by one out to Dollie Finch's car. O what a night! And we had champagne at Birdie's!'

'Birdie Bernstein,' said Thomas laying about him to the window-seat, 'Dollie Finch.'

'Dollie Finch,' said Mrs. McMenamin, joining him, 'Birdie Bernstein.'

'Birdie Bernstein was once bitten on the behind by a police-dog,' said Packy, taking the last place on the window-seat.

App arranged bottles and glasses on a too-small table. Roddy sat at the feet of Mrs. McMenamin and gloomed at her. Primrose squatted against Packy's knee and pretended she didn't feel the deliberate pressure on her spine.

'Dollie Finch,' said Packy, 'once stole a police-car.'

'A very fine woman,' said Thomas.

App had taken up his position by the mantlepiece on which there were signed photographs of Queen Marie of Rumania, Ivor Novello, Mistinguett, and Alfred Byrne, T.D., many times Lord Mayor of Dublin. Already that night App had lost his temper twice explaining to the Past Pupils who these people were.

'Leah,' crooned App, 'you know everybody.'

'I do not,' she growled.

'Of course you do,' he gonged. 'All except Buttercup there who thinks you're my mammy.'

'Let me at her,' Leah said absently. She did not move.

Whisking, whisking, staring straight ahead at a photograph of Nugent App in a leopard-skin loin-cloth.

'Tell me App,' said Thomas, above the humming of the Past Pupils, 'where were you born?'

'Now it's funny you should ask me that. I remember Jean Cocteau asking me exactly the same question when I was a very young man in Paris and I said "Why do you ask?" and he said "Because you have a face, not English, but *vraiment celtique*" and after that he took me to see Mistinguett ...'

'Mistinguett me granny,' said Thomas. 'Where were you born?'

'And she said practically the same thing and I said of course I'm not English but Irish, of Cornish and Manx extraction ...'

'Where were you born?' said Thomas, minatory.

'As a matter of fact I was born on the Liverpool boat so I could claim to be English if I wanted to, but not after 1916 and all that. I remember Douglas Hyde saying to me — An Chraoibhinn Aoibhinn you know — saying to me in his lovely garden at French Park, *"A Nugent a thaisge,* you have chosen the good portion".'

'Jean Cocteau,' said Thomas, stupefied. 'Mistinguett, Douglas Hyde.'

'Those murals by Cocteau in the French Church at Leicester Square,' said Packy authoritatively, 'are very sound.'

'Birdie Bernstein, Dollie Finch,' said Thomas.

The humming seemed to have grown louder, and it was some time before anyone grasped that a new burden had been struck up, a harsh yap-gulp sound, some animal in labour perhaps, but devastatingly human. For it was Leah struggling with tears such as Titanesses weep, and she advanced like a tank on Nugent App.

'Goats and monkeys,' she pronounced carefully. The bees stopped. 'All the perfumes of Arabia could not sweeten that little soul.'

'She's drunk,' said App amiably.

'App,' she said, 'you are a traitor to your peoples.'

'Go to bed, cream-in-my-coffee,' said App. He had begun

to shake.

'App,' she said, 'you are a Jew and you were born in the
Ghetto of Warsaw where your poppa and momma died and
your brother Jan was shot by the pig-Germans.'

'Aaaaaah,' moaned App. 'What a scene before the Past
Pupils.'

'App,' she said, 'it is you that are drunk. You are drunk
from lying and cheating and the fear that I'll die and leave
you alone for a dirty old man.'

'Stop.'

'I am going to study the Works of Shakespeare,' she said.
'There I will find peace,' and she moved from the room like a
mobile pillar.

'A decenter woman never shat,' said Thomas.

She did so decently before entering into her cave for
peace. She locked the door and she stuffed a sheep-skin rug
into the slit between her and the world of App. She did not
have to shut the window. Carefully, with massive
movements, she lit her gas-fire. She poured out a tumbler of
gin, and with a great sigh-grunt settled herself in her basket-
chair. She adjusted herself to pick up the Works of
Shakespeare, opened them and read,

The blind mole casts
Copp'd hills towards heaven, to tell the earth is throng'd
By man's oppression; and the poor worm doth die for't.

The mammoth tears began again. 'Man's oppression,' she
groaned. She trundled to her desk and took out her bottle of
aspirin. Ten, maybe fifteen, she swallowed and drowned
them in gin. She turned off the gas-fire, turned it on again,
did not light it. She took more gin, and the gathering fumes
were mild as Abraham leaned to clasp this child to his
bosom. She was dropping off into a muddled dream of
Nugent App and he was saying, *Liebchen, Liebchen,* love,
love, love will conquer all.

'Cross old Leah,' App was saying. 'I'd better go and fetch
her.'

'Surely,' said Thomas, 'I'm convinced she'd know far more about elephants than you.'

'You're a renegade,' said Packy sternly.

'She's too good for you,' said Primrose, 'even if she's your mother.'

'It's not quite the same when you lose your mother,' said Mrs. McMenamin.

The Past Pupils were in each others arms, boy and girl curled tranquilly together, passionless, silent, out of this world. A skinny archangel shot up and ever-conscious of the Art of Noble Speech, trumpeted, 'Gas'.

App skiltered to the door, and they heard the knocking and the howls of the damned.

'She turned on the gas,' said Thomas. 'She turned on the gas'.

'Get up to bed, Rose,' said Roddy.

'I couldn't possibly appear at an inquest,' said Packy.

'A man that married his mother,' said Primrose.

'It's a black day for me,' said Thomas.

But when the knocking and the howling had ceased and like cattle they bumped out to the hall, it was Leah, puce, mad-eyed, vomiting, who held App in her arms as he fought against dying from the loss of his mother-wife. Perhaps some sliver of memory about Belsen or Buchenwald had gashed Leah's stupor, and on her forehead was an ugly cross where she'd hit herself turning off the gas.

'The poor bastard,' said Thomas.

The phone rang. Roddy answered. It was Dollie Finch and she said she was coming round. He put the phone down and rang for a doctor and a priest, for App, though of no known religion, had been seen on Sundays in the Pro-Cathedral. He remembered to ring for a Gárda only after Birdie Bernstein had rung up to say she was coming round.

An ambulance took away Leah and App. The Gárda took statements. The Past Pupils took taxis home. Thomas, Rose, Packy, Primrose and Roddy, took the remaining drink upstairs.

But the late dawn saw them distributed each to his own nightmare. Packy took Primrose with him, and at six o'clock she was saying, 'One hour together and you're asleep.'

'Down, Primrose, down,' said Packy. Roddy watched by the bed of Mrs. McMenamin and noted greedily the fragments of her sleep-talk. 'It's not quite the same,' she said loudly, and snored. 'Heart love gas,' she mumbled, and whistled. 'I'll sing a hymn to Mary,' she hummed, and snorted. He had never felt nearer to her.

And in his room Thomas had a drink of Scotch and infinitely weary sat down to his typewriter. His head was full of beasts, of drunken elephants, and performing bears, and mice and poodles and goats and monkeys, and poor human trash.

Tango

It was half-past five and the bar was beginning to fill. And it was Friday, the day when Tango began to feel kicks of anticipation before the week-end. Mid-week parties, even mid-week conquests, were no more than tentative rehearsals for the party of parties, the love that would surpass all other loves, to be looked for at week-ends. On these Fridays, Tango was accustomed to decide that life was very beautiful, and that the world, for all its horrors, contained many very beautiful people, so many beautiful people that now Tango's head swam just a little. There was, for instance, that boy he had met at Laurie Casey's, so young dear, and yet so intelligent. To-morrow they would have dinner together, and discuss the Ballet, perhaps, or Evelyn Waugh — Waugh was always a nice safe bet since Penguin had done him — and after, they would go on, he hoped, to Issy's party at Ballycodder, and then, who knew? All the beauty in the world, thought Tango, and the little of it that wished to be loved more than made up for the very great deal that did not — but Issy's voice drilled through his reverie, and he was back on his high stool, facing the lovely convenient mirrors, his hand tight about gin-and-tonic.

'The trouble with my parties,' Issy Bell was saying, 'is that too many gutthersnipes have been crashin' in. What we want is a bit of class. I've a very nice English lad comin' along, and I don't want him to think we can't do things as well as they do them in London.'

Usually genial, Mr. Bell was now obviously in a bad

humour. His heart of gold had had many demands made on it recently: American sailors who took their clothes off at an unreasonably early hour, a Government clerk who had fallen out of the bathroom window and broken his arm, worst of all a literary man who had created uproar by bringing along his mistress and several of his newspaper cronies. As he said on that occasion, Dublin was fast becoming a place where a man couldn't call his house his own.

He ordered another Smithwick, and scowling at the urinish dregs at the bottom of his glass, continued, 'I've always tried to maintain a certain standhard of culthur at my country house, but in a place like Dublin it's very hard to keep out gutties.'

'Issy darling,' said Tango, 'you don't really *mean* that.'

'I certainly do.'

'But darling, gutties are sometimes so *nice*. And, *usually,* the intellectual ones are so dull. They've got brains, I suppose, but very little else that *you'd* be interested in.'

'I don't know watcher mean,' said Bell aggressively. 'I'm interested in opera and ballet and picthures. I'm buildin' up a very good collection.'

'Yes, Issy dear,' and Tango smoothed back his hair. He looked absently into the mirrors behind the bar. No-one in sight worth turning on his stool for. But the gray at your temples is rather distinguished dear, he thought.

'I like to know where people come from,' said Mr. Bell. 'Good family always has a certain standhard of culthur.'

'Aha dear, I see you have the Morris Minor down on your list. Does he come up to your standards?'

'He doesn't matther,' said Mr. Bell. 'Anyway he has to come if Henry Martin comes.'

Tango's head had stopped swimming. I feel very well dear, he told himself. He looked roguishly at Mr. Bell and said,

'And where do the Bells come from, Issy darling?'

He was flabbergasted by the reply.

'We come from Leitrim,' said Mr. Bell savagely.

Tango ought to have known better than to press the point, but the fifth gin had done its work, and he did. Besides to-day was to-day, and there was always to-morrow, and that nice piece he'd met at Laurie Casey's, and the week-end ahead dear, and Christmas coming too ... catching himself up in a pleasant vision of snow, mistletoe and unending love, he bent over to Mr. Bell. His carefully shaved face relaxed into the mask of an old Irish mother, tough and kindly, gently glowing from the spiritual sauna of a million rosaries, gently sad from a million nights of lying awake in prayer for her children in Liverpool and Boston, gently tolerant from dealing with a million drunken spouses who had more (but not much more) money than sense.

'God bless you Issy,' he said. 'But "Leitrim" now? I remember when you lived on the canal, ah yes, because I was living with my Gran on the other side, and I can see as if it was to-day, you helping your da to unload his rickety old hand-cart — "Auld Candle-Butt Bell" the kids used to call him, because he used to collect candle-ends and melt them down, God Himself knows why — and ah yes I remember the ice on the canal in winter, and you — ah Issy love do you remember? — with your poor red hands all goin' purple from bein' out with your da, but my Gran had knitted me a pair of lovely green wool gloves, and a green scarf, and God they were grand in the cold weather.'

The little Irish mother had become a gay young girl again and Tango's eyes wettened as he hit upon a new dream-life, and he saw himself as he rushed along the canal, plaits flying, green scarf streaming, an adorable tomboy.

'We come from Leitrim,' said Mr. Bell firmly. 'The Bells of Leitrim are a very well-known family.'

'Yes dear.' And now the tomboy had grown up and there was too much washing to be done, and too many babies, and a husband always on for you know what, and the dress from the bargain basement too tight after all.

Tango's silence was taken as retreat by Mr. Bell. It occurred to him to question the existence, then or at any other time, of Tango's Gran, but decided it was better to carry on with the business of guest-weeding.

'That Purcell fella is too clever,' he said. 'You never know what he's thinkin'. I'm often afraid he's no more than a snooper. He might write a book, and that wouldn't do at all.'

He ordered another Smithwick and a gin-and-tonic for Tango.

'And Henry Martin can only bring the Morris Minor. But we might tell him to tip off that boy from Indo-China.'

'He's from Trinidad dear,' said Tango gently.

'He's from Indo-China.'

'No dear he's from Trinidad.'

Mr. Bell's face passed from dough to salmon.

'I said, he's from Indo-China. I had a very interestin' conversation with him about Indo-China.'

'That may well be,' said Tango, in a familiar we-are-not-pleased voice. 'But anyway dear, what do *you* know about Indo-China?'

'I know a good amount about Indo-China,' said Mr. Bell. 'And I've had enough of this bargyin'. I have to meet a well-known Dublin lawyer for dinner. That boy from England's comin' along too, and I mustn't be late.'

Half-way to the door he pulled around and a large smile opened on his face, which was dough again. His eyes, deep-set and porched, were friendly once more.

'Of course *you'll* be along on Saturday night, won't you?'

Tango nodded with precision and dignity. He must not appear too eager. But he knew well that without him, the party at Ballycodder might well go flat. They love you so much, dear, he said to the mirror, because they know you're a romantic survival dear, that you believe that the world and people are so beautiful if only one *takes* them the right way.

'Yes dear I'll be there and —,' hand cocked, eyes twinkling, eyebrows raised naughtily, 'be careful about your nationalities. Some of them are so touchy dear. Remember it's Trinidad, not Indo-China.'

But Mr. Bell had gone out into the dark. Now, thought Tango, now for the birds in this nice warm cage. They were gathering. He got off his stool, squared his shoulders and walked slowly down the bar. A young man in a blazer said 'Hello, sir.' Tango stared pityingly at him.

'My boy,' he said, 'as long as you're a friend of mine, never call me "sir". But you *may* address me as "madam".'

Then running the young man over without much interest, he turned back to the counter. It wasn't a very good night. But later, he would come back and look around again. You never know dear, he said into the remains of his gin-and-tonic, *when* Me is likely to turn up.

He finished his drink, turned up his collar and pulled down his hat. But the news-vendor outside the door imagined for a moment that he sold the evening paper to some old one from Rathgar, so great was the disdain, so aloof the face, so refined and Protestant the voice. A less prejudiced observer might have seen an Anglo-Irish gentlewoman of fine carriage and an air of exceptional breeding, cross the street carefully, and get into a dinky little *coupé*. That class liked a glass of sherry in a respectable pub, after a hard day's shopping.

.   .   .   .

Not since the early days in London had Tango felt so happy. He was merry, fully lucid, and yet could still feel the after-dinner brandy and the post-brandy pub gins mingling at where his tonsils used to be. The *coupé* was going like a bird, the night was clear and moonlit, and Alec, dear Alec, was breathing contentedly beside him.

'Make a wish dear,' he whispered dramatically. And he cocked his eye at the moon, a blurred ball of honey through the frosted windscreen. Tango thought of one of his childhoods, when he had spent all night watching the moon through the little mad sketches with which Jack Frost had covered the window, until his father came in, drunk as a newt, to give him one of his big slobbery kisses. He had taken him up in his arms from the window-seat and even now Tango could feel the hot wet hands round his legs and shoulder-blades, and the baby hairs on his calf seeming to sprout.

'Have you made it, dear boy?' asked Tango.

'I have,' said Alec. He wore soiled brown corduroys, a leather-wristed and elbowed jacket, and his shoes needed polishing. But after all, thought Tango, most students are like that, in Ireland anyway. And he'd never got on very well with students from England, though he admired their nice

drainpipe trousers, and many of their waistcoats were
unquestionably Me.

Alec was remembering how amusing Tango had been at
dinner, though he wished he'd remembered to put on his best
suit. Tango didn't seem to mind. All in all, he was a grand
type. He couldn't really bring himself to believe the stories
about Tango he'd heard from some of the boys . . . but he
would know what to do if Tango tried any monkey business.
He'd heard of two fellows on the quays, who'd kicked one of
Tango's kind in the stomach, when he tried fooling with them
in a jax. Or rather the kind they said Tango was. He'd never
be able to kick Tango, but when he wished to the moon
through glass, it was that nothing like that would happen.

Tango began to sing, in a high soft voice,

'I know where I'm going,
And I know who's going with me.'

They passed several cars, all, probably, on their way to
Ballycodder. Soon they had left the main road and were
climbing up the mountain. Tall hedges shut away the fields
on either side. The road became a dirt-track and the hedges
straggled away. It was so quiet that the murmur of the *coupé*
and Tango's humming seemed to Alec to be the last sounds
left in the world. He thought of the boys, huddled over a
dozen of stout in someone's digs, singing dirty songs in a
half-whisper for fear the landlady would kick up a row, and
sank deeper into his seat.

'The stars,' said Tango, 'aren't they marvellous?' and
began to sing again,

'I have stockings of silk
And shoes of fine green leather.'

They passed a white-washed cottage looking lemon in the
moonlight, nearly knocked down an old man who had
crossed the road to urinate, laughed together when the old
man let out a screech of rage, and looked at each other to
share their laughter more fully. Tango tasted something like
chocolate at the back of his throat. Another childhood
surfaced. There was a river bank, a reflection of fawn-
coloured reeds, cold sunlight, boys bathing, and one of them
undressing under a mackintosh, the squelching sound as the

mackintosh was thrown off and trodden into the soaking-wet grass. Tango changed gear, and thought of the night to come at Ballycodder, darling Issy presiding over his piles of sandwiches and rows of bottles, the illusion of never-endingness, as it got on for three, or maybe four or five in the morning.

He turned the car in off the track to a rutted drive. A low squat house was ahead of them, lit up like a cinema, surrounded by cars. The door was open, and as they drew up, a low squat figure blocked the hall-way. Mr. Bell was doing all the honours the evening.

'Issy dear this is *Alec.*'

'I'm very pleased to meetcher,' said Mr. Bell. He shook Alec's hand in the way he might have pulled a lavarory chain.

'Come on in and have a drink. There's a lot of very nice people here. Henry Martin, and Fintan Foley, and Alfred Baxter the well-known Dublin lawyer.'

Mr. Bell held his parties in a large room which he used on other occasions as a study. Constant experience had not taught him that valuables of any kind were best removed before parties. His own portrait, by a distinguished Irish academician, had several times received glasses of stout full in the face. There were gaps in his shelves of first editions. His library of *erotica* had been plundered frequently, and on one occasion a bust of Beethoven had been shattered, by a drunk young man who said he couldn't see what *that* was doing there. Mr. Bell had taken this remark as a reflection both on his taste in busts and on his standards of culture in general, and the young man was not again invited. But Beethoven had not been replaced.

This evening there were about a dozen men in the room, of whom half were grouped around a middle-aged man with a bald head and a cigar, who was talking excitedly about Africa.

'I'll introduce you in a moment dear boy,' Tango whispered to Alec. 'It's Henry Martin, he's *travelled* a lot.'

'D'you know,' said Henry Martin, 'it's a curious thing, but whenever I think about Africa — of course I mean South

Africa — I remember a little place in Johannesburg where
you could always get the most wonderful game pie.'

He looked anxiously at a young man in a brown velvet
suit, who looked as if he might be about to interpolate.

'And, as you know, I don't go in for food much, unless it's
well cooked. But do you know, you could get a damn good
meal at that place for — oh I suppose about ten bob.'

'How much?' asked the young man in brown velvet.

'Oh ten or fifteen bob.'

'Some people might think that quite a lot.'

'Now, now,' said Henry Martin, 'don't rag me Fintan dear
boy —'

He had just noticed Tango. Alec heard him distinctly say
'Christ' under his breath. With one hand held out, the other
pressed to an invisible corsage, Tango did his famous
London hostess number.

'Henry my dear, how nice to see you.'

'Tango, it's been a damn long time, where have you been
— not I hope getting involved again with Uncle Sam's boys?'

Tango took this comment amiss. He accepted, with the air
of one who is trying to conceal awareness of a bad smell, the
large gin which Mr. Bell had brought him.

'Introduce us to your friend, Tango, there's a dear,' said
the young man in brown velvet.

'Henry Martin, Fintan Foley, Alfred Baxter . . .' Alec lost
track of the names. Mr. Bell had brought him gin too, and
Alec thought again of the boys, emptying out the drains from
the dozen of stout. Alec found himself talking to the young
man called Fintan Foley, who had shrewd cold eyes and a
lot of blonde hair.

'Have you known Tango long?' asked Foley.

'I met him a few days ago at a party — Laurie Casey's
party — do you know her?'

'Indeed I do,' Foley sighed theatrically. 'That one has
what's coming to her.'

Alec was embarrassed.

'I think she's a nice woman, I mean she's pretty generous.'

'Yes,' said Foley. 'Like Tango.'

Alec was relieved when Foley turned to Henry Martin.

'Look Henry,' he said gently, 'Martha and Mary are in attendance again.'

'Christ,' roared Henry Martin.

'No dear,' said Foley. 'Just dear little Larry Morris.'

Alec trailed along after Foley and Henry Martin to a group of three who were standing by the mantlepiece under Mr. Bell's portrait. Tango crossed the room and joined them. 'The one talking is the Morris Minor, you know the crooner, Larry Morris,' he whispered to Alec. Larry Morris was holding the floor. His attendants were a carrot-haired man of uncertain age, and a juvenile of twenty-seven or so, with what Alec took to be a better-class kind of London accent. Morris was talking about George Eliot.

'Henry there,' he pointed to him, 'is makin' me read the "great Victorians" as he calls them. I'm bored up to me eyebrows. If you ask me, that Eliot one was a proper dike.'

'Oh come now,' said Henry Martin. 'Why do you say that?'

'Well look at her takin' a man's name . . .'

Alec felt himself being pulled away by Tango, just as Henry Martin began to explain the position of women novelists in the nineteenth century. But Mr. Bell drew Tango away into a corner, and Alec found himself again with Fintan Foley.

'Lovely party,' Foley said coldly.

'Yes, it's grand, though I don't often go to this kind of party.'

'This kind of party?'

'Well, I mean, you don't often see people like Larry Morris at the parties I go to. And there's generally a couple of girls,' he noticed that Foley's eyebrows went up, 'and dancing.'

'Oh, there'll be dancing, never fear.'

Mr. Bell at this point clapped his hands, and despite protests from Tango, whose advice he had asked, and as usual not taken, announced that — 'Everyone knows Rupert, I suppose' — had very kindly agreed to give an improvised mime.

'So silence,' said Mr. Bell, 'while Rupert does a little mime

to the lovely music of Debussy's *Afthernoon of a Faun.*' Alec
was embarrassed for the very large young man who came
into the centre of the room. He heard Henry Martin say that
the boy couldn't *move* for toffee, let alone mime, but that he
remembered a first-class artist in Copenhagen ... He saw
Fintan Foley slip out of the room with an intent expression,
and behind Mr. Bell, Tango was making faces, ranging from
that of a distraught guide-mistress to that of a tragedy queen
compelled to take to the halls.   All of these faces were well
known to Mr. Bell's guests, but Alec found them wonderfully
new and funny.

The young man who was to mime, took off his coat, and a
voice asked was that all. Mr. Bell fiddled with the
phonograph, and Rupert began to make obscure frantic
movements with his arms and hips. The guests were for the
most part quiet during the performance, and Mr. Bell placed
his hands on his stomach and never looked more genial. But
the applause was scattered and Mr. Bell looked around
fiercely for commendations of his *protégé.*

'Lovely, dear boy, lovely,' said Henry Martin.

'You should take it up, dear,' said Larry Morris.

'I'm old-fashioned,' said Tango.

A man whose physique had impressed Alec greatly,
suddenly shrieked,

'Let's have some *real* dancing'.

'Boys will be boys,' said Tango.

'I wonder why the boy from England hasn't showed up,'
said Mr. Bell. 'He has his own car,' he added affectionately.

The record for dancing was *Always.* Tango considered
asking Alec for the pleasure, but thought better of it.

'How romantic that tune is,' he said. 'Don't you think so?'

'I don't know,' said Mr. Bell. 'I prefer a bit of classical
music.'

'Aha dear. You're getting hide-bound in your old age.'

'I was forty-one last birthday,' said Mr. Bell threateningly.

'Tell that to some of those nice Dutch marines you had
down last summer. And breathe it not in Baggot Street dear,
I'm forty-one myself.'

 'Well?'

'Well dear I remember you when you were quite a big boy
when I was a little fellow and lived with my Gran ...'

'I'm sick to death hearing about your Gran and ...'

He might have gone on, were it not that the long-awaited
boy from England arrived at this moment.

'Silence,' said Mr. Bell. The dancers stopped, the
phonograph was shut off, and Mr. Bell led a very drunk
young man into the middle of the room.

'This,' said Mr. Bell, 'is a very good friend of mine.'

'I don't doubt it,' said Fintan Foley.

Mr. Bell ignored him.

'David here is from across the water, and we must see he
has a good time.'

'He'll have it,' said Fintan Foley.

The dancing was resumed and the party went on for a
time without any further interruption. Tango went from
couple to couple and group to group, a gay youthful light in
his eyes, never quite losing sight of Alec, who was listening
respectfully to Henry Martin telling stories about what had
happened to him in Bulgarian hotels. There he is, thought
Tango, there he is. His eyes began to swim with happy
affectionate tears.

The room was now nearly twice as full as it was when
they arrived. Newcomers were quickly absorbed into the
dancing, or the groups who observed from corners. Tango
noticed suddenly that something was wrong in the group
where Mr. Bell had inserted his friend David. He saw Fintan
Foley reach for a large bull-rush out of a *famille verte* jar on
a side-table, and just as the record being played came to an
end, he saw Foley begin to beat David across the face with
the bull-rush, patiently and rhythmically.

'How *dare* you,' he was saying in a loud voice, 'come here
and bore *us* for so long, and so successfully.'

'Lookit here', began Mr. Bell, but stopped, appalled, as the
Morris Minor handed another bullrush to Foley.

'Hit her again dear. Hit the dreary queen again.'

Mr. Bell's face passed from dough via green to salmon,
before going purple.

'Such conduct,' he thundered. 'If this hooliganism doesn't

stop, the party will *finish*.'

He glared at Foley and the Morris Minor, took the
weeping David by the hand, and led him into a corner. For
some time afterwards he was heard assuring David that he
was a very nice lad, and not to mind the boys. They were a
bit sharp sometimes, but had very good hearts.

Another guest arriving at last drew Mr. Bell away from
David, who was immediately taken over by Alfred Baxter,
the well-known Dublin lawyer. The newcomer was a
coloured young man, whom Mr. Bell led forward with the
light of battle in his porched eyes.

'I'm sorry I'm so late,' said the coloured young man. 'I
couldn't get a lift out, so if you don't mind, I've a friend who
was kind enough to drive me out, would you mind — ?'

'Of course not,' said Mr. Bell jovially. 'Bring him in.'

The coloured young man called out 'Jim' and a wide-eyed
youth whom Alec recognized as a medical student from his
college, stepped into the room suspiciously.

'Xavier and Jim,' said Mr. Bell. 'Join the party.'

'You're from Trinidad, aren't you?' said Tango.

'He's from Siam,' said Larry Morris.

'I thought he came from Burma,' said Henry Martin. 'He
reminds me . . .'

'Xavier is from Indo-China,' said Mr. Bell triumphantly.

'I'm from Trinidad,' said Xavier.

'Aha,' said Tango, with straight back and gimlet eyes, a
mathematics mistress detecting the ugliest girl in the class at
copying, 'I thought so.'

Mr. Bell ignored the correction, and steered Xavier to the
recovered David. Later in the evening, Tango noticed that
Xavier and David had grown very friendly. The dark grave
face nodded sympathetically as David talked on and on, and
by two o'clock David had placed his hand on Xavier's knee.
Tango looked around for Alec.

.   .   .   .

It was cool in the kitchen. The party was still going on,
but as Mr. Bell had suddenly had a desire to hear Puccini, all
that Tango and Alec could hear from the study was the

muted voice of some Butterfly. Tango tensed to the sweet,
easy melody, and leaning across the kitchen table where he
and Alec sat picking at a round of cold beef, he smiled sadly
and said,

'You know, little man, I'm very fond of you.'

'Yes, yes, thank you, Tango.'

Alec was not feeling well. He could remember little about
the last hour or so, except that a thin milky substance had
formed on the lips of the well-known Dublin lawyer,
Alfred Baxter, just before he collapsed on the floor, babbling
that he'd have them all, he'd have them all; and that the man
whose physique Alec had admired, had had his jaw punched
by Jim the medical student: he could hear Jim now saying in
a thick brogue, that he'd met this kind of thing before,
though not in Galway, and knew how to deal with it. Alec
began to doze, and Tango laid his hand on his arm with
great gentleness. Mr. Bell evidently thought a lot of *One Fine
Day,* for it had begun again. Tango was at a loss as to which
childhood to settle on, as he sat looking at Alec's slumped
face. But gradually the taste of chocolate overcame that of
brandy and gin, as it had done in the car, and to his distress,
he was on the river bank again and the sound of mackintosh
being trodden into the soaking-wet grass prevailed over the
sounds of all the other childhoods, and even Mr. Bell's
prima donna.

'Little man,' he said.

Alec's eyes opened, and Tango smiled in a way intended
to crack the glaze which was rapidly growing more
noticeable.

'Little man,' he said, 'I feel great *affection* for you.'

'Yes.'

'Little man, we must see more of each other.'

By now, thought Alec, the dozen empty bottles would be
piled back in their sugar bags, and the boys would be in bed.

'Yes I'd like that,' said Alec.

'I mean, we could *get on* together.'

'How do you mean Tango?'

'Well, we could —'

'Tango, I feel sick.'

'Ah dear boy, that's easily seen to. *Come* along.'

Tango led Alec out through the back door, pointed to a clump of bushes, and said,

'That way dear, there's a sort of outdoor place for getting sick. Issy's very particular about that sort of thing.'

'It's all right, you needn't come, Tango.'

'But I'm *worried,* dear boy, I mean —'

'I'm not sick any longer,' snapped Alec.

'But that's marvellous, dear boy.'

'And I know what you're up to, you bloody cissy.'

'How *dare* you, how *dare* you speak to me like that.'

It had begun to rain, the moon had clouded, and Tango could barely see Alec's face. But he saw enough to know that love had been foiled. So, in the darkness, a great lady of the *ancien régime* faced her accusers, and moved them by the patent sincerity of her disavowals.

'I am sorry that you should misunderstand me.'

'I've got to go home.'

'I offer you my friendship, and you give me vulgar abuse in return.'

'I'm sorry I ever came here, you'd no right to bring me to a party like this'.

'I do not know what you mean.'

'Ah stop cod-actin'.'

'I think you'd better find your own way home. Perhaps that medical friend of yours will take you.'

Alec had gone.

Tango turned back, head held high, and with his arms straight at his side. The rain fell heavily on his bare head and he made a mental note to tidy himself up before going back to the party. In the kitchen again he decided he needed a quiet drink by himself, before joining the others. From experience he knew that he would find a bottle of brandy in the pantry. Now pull yourself together dear, he told himself, as he poured a large tot into a water-glass. Remember to leave well alone, and anyway, it was really rather a dreary piece. What if he'd got sick in the flat? Tango braced himself against the picturesque invective of his housekeeper, saw his profile pained and oddly touching in the mirror over his fireplace, so obviously not a face made to deal with quarrelsome retainers.

He sat down by the table, bottle in one hand, glass in the other, listened to the rain pelting on the pantry skylight, and gradually they gathered about him, the adoring invisible of the world. They were there, and always would be there, the rows and rows of grateful faces of those who appreciated wit and courage and the endless capacity for love. The silent applause engulfed Tango, knocked at his heart, brought tears to his eyes. He poured another large tot, and as the pounding in his chest grew more violent, and the tears dribbled over his cheeks, his profile slipped out of focus, and his fingers began to stick to his glass. Pull yourself together dear, he said aloud, remember, they're watching.

He got up briskly, ruffled his hair so that it looked as if the wind had played in it, and finished his brandy. Back to the visible, vaguely treacherous audience, where somehow one was never prepared for the cat-call, the ugly gallery unbelief.

Mr. Bell's guests were far gone in drink, but they paused, nonetheless, to stare at this stranger who came into the room. Who was this rueful-looking boy who slipped in so quietly, with the air of one who has just been chastened by his first experience of unhappy loving?

'Tango,' they all said. 'We've missed you so much.'